"What time is it, Patrick?"

Carly stretched luxuriously as she spoke. She couldn't remember ever being so happy.

"Late. It's almost time to leave for the office." He ran a possessive hand over her thigh as he gazed down at her. "I've been watching you sleep."

"That couldn't have been much fun."

"On the contrary. You're very beautiful, Carly Ashton." He leaned over to kiss the peak of her breast, teasing it with his tongue. "Absolutely exquisite."

"How . . . how late are we?" she asked, suddenly breathless.

He smiled warmly, lazily. "Not *that* late . . ."

JoAnn Ross didn't set out to write a trilogy when she first started working on *Magic in the Night*. But as the writing progressed, she became more and more intrigued with her secondary character, Alex Bedare. His story cried out to be told. The heartwarming result, *Playing for Keeps*, will be published in January 1987.

JoAnn is currently finishing the third book of this delightful series, focusing on Donovan, sexy brother of the heroine in *Playing for Keeps*. Also featured is a gorilla named Gloria!

Books by JoAnn Ross

HARLEQUIN TEMPTATION

These books may be available at your local bookseller.

Don't miss any of our special offers. Write to us at the following address for information on our newest releases.

Harlequin Reader Service
901 Fuhrmann Blvd., P.O. Box 1397, Buffalo, NY 14240
Canadian address: P.O. Box 603,
Fort Erie, Ont. L2A 9Z9

Magic in the Night

JoAnn Ross

Harlequin Books

TORONTO • NEW YORK • LONDON
AMSTERDAM • PARIS • SYDNEY • HAMBURG
STOCKHOLM • ATHENS • TOKYO • MILAN

Published October 1986

ISBN 0-373-25226-9

1

IT WAS DEFINITELY NOT your usual opening conversational gambit. Still, once she had squelched her impulse to knock that arrogant expression off the stranger's face, Carly Ashton had to admit the tall, dark-haired man standing over her had captured her attention.

"Excuse me?"

"I asked if you're the little lady McIntyre's throwing in to sweeten the pot." His gaze flicked over her in a detached, mocking way. "If so, things are certainly looking up."

Carly had lived in Washington, D.C., for seven years without experiencing any street crime. Although she refused to shrink from his silent study, she suddenly felt as though she'd been expertly mugged. And the amazing thing about it, Carly considered with reluctant admiration, was that her assailant had managed to pull it off without a blink of those hooded blue eyes.

"I'm afraid you have me confused with someone else," she replied icily, before returning her attention to her companion. "Now, Bill, what were you saying?"

The intruder appeared unperturbed by her dismissal. "You are Carly Ashton, aren't you?" Carly's irritation rose to new heights as he settled uninvited into a chair across the small table from her.

"That's right," she agreed, tossing her dark blond hair over her shoulder with an impatient gesture.

"Patrick Ryan," he introduced himself.

"Oh, yes. The man who's come all the way down from the big city to put us out of business." Carly didn't bother to conceal her contempt for both the man and his mission.

Bill McIntyre squirmed uncomfortably. "Carly," her partner warned under his breath, "I invited Mr. Ryan here tonight for a get-acquainted drink."

Out of the corner of her eye, Carly viewed a deep flush rising above the collar of Bill's silk shirt. His florid complexion was due to a combination of high blood pressure and embarrassment, and she knew her hostile attitude was not making things easy on him. But Patrick Ryan had insinuated that there was more to be had here tonight than a simple drink, and she was furious at being put in such a position.

"I'm sure Mr. Ryan knows all about us, Bill. After all, he's been investigating Capitol Airlines for the past three months." She allowed a cool, ingratiating smile, ignoring Bill's pointed cough. "Surely you have enough information to make a decision on whether we're worth your while by now, Mr. Ryan."

Patrick returned her smile with one that didn't quite reach his eyes. "I make it a habit never to make a snap decision, Ms Ashton," he replied easily. "Just as I never depend on dry documents and figures alone." His eyes darkened wickedly as they settled momentarily on her lips. "I prefer a more personal approach to my business dealings."

"Interesting," Carly mused aloud, running a fingernail around the rim of her glass. "It's been a while since I spent any time in a biology class, but I distinctly remember learning that the shark is a cold-blooded animal."

Patrick silently gave her points for not backing down. "A reformed shark, Ms Ashton," he corrected softly.

Carly sighed inwardly, deciding that Bill was probably right. There was no point in antagonizing the man. After all, he was the only hope they had. Although she hated the idea of a takeover, at least it was better than closing shop or being gobbled up by one of the major airlines. Patrick Ryan might not resemble a white knight but at this point he was all they had.

Patrick realized he'd lost her. "Ms Ashton?"

Carly shook her head to clear it of these depressing thoughts. "I'm sorry—my mind was wandering. What did you say?"

Patrick observed that her hands were never idle; for a time her fingers had circled the rim of her martini glass, and now they were absently stroking the stem.

"I simply suggested that your information might be a bit out of date; that label no longer fits. I promise you, Ms Ashton," he tacked on wickedly, "I'm a great deal more warm-blooded than my reputation suggests."

Carly could not miss the innuendo in his tone. The restaurant was as noisy as ever, the room packed with the usual contingent of politicians, lobbyists, congressional aides, reporters and political groupies. But as Patrick suddenly smiled at her, they could have been the only two people in the room. Her mind went into high gear as she attempted to come up with a blistering response. But as hard as she tried, Carly came up blank.

She was relieved when the unnerving hum of sexual tension was suddenly shattered by the maître d' announcing a telephone call for Bill. The older man jumped up from the table, looking as if he'd just escaped the hangman.

"I'll be right back," he assured them both. "Carly, order Mr. Ryan a drink."

Carly and Patrick watched Bill make his way through the crowd at the bar to the telephone.

"That's part of your problem," Patrick murmured.

"What's part of my problem?" she asked, watching his mouth twist derisively. His lips were too firmly chiseled for her taste, hinting at a hard, unyielding character. And his blue eyes resembled twin glaciers.

"McIntyre, of course. It's no wonder Capitol Airlines is drowning in red ink, the way he's been running the place the past two years."

"I don't know what you're talking about, Mr. Ryan."

"Come on, Ms Ashton," Patrick objected. "You are admittedly an intelligent woman, but you're a lousy liar."

Carly thoughtfully sipped her drink, remembering the conversation she and Bill had shared before Patrick Ryan's arrival at the restaurant.

"I still can't figure out what we're doing here tonight," she had complained. "Surely Monday morning is soon enough to meet the infamous Mr. Ryan."

"Monday he's coming to the office," Bill had countered. "Monocle's a more congenial atmosphere. I thought it would be a good idea to get a little groundwork done before we get down to business."

Something in his tone alerted Carly. "What do you mean?"

Bill averted his eyes, unwilling to meet her suddenly sharp gaze. "He should be here any minute."

"Bill," Carly insisted, "answer my question."

His expression was unmistakably guilty as he slowly, reluctantly looked at her. "Try to see it my way," he pleaded, his voice thick with desperation. "Everything I own is tied up in Capitol. If it goes down, I go. Can you understand what that will do to me? To my life?"

Carly thought of Bill's wife, Elaine, who sought to assuage her own pain by embarking on shopping sprees with the same energy knights of old expended in searching for the Holy Grail. Although Bill remained closemouthed about his daughter's accident, Carly knew Meredith's medical bills had to be astronomical. Not to mention the upkeep on his house in fashionable Chevy Chase, a horse farm in Virginia, and that mansion the McIntyres called their "summer cottage" on Hilton Head.

He had a great deal to lose. But Bill wasn't the only one who would suffer if the airline folded. Carly had invested everything she had in the business, as well.

"I know," she answered sympathetically. "But we're in this together. All the way."

Bill's eyes brightened considerably as Carly seemed to be softening. He patted her hand in a fond, paternalistic way, at the same time giving her a warm, guileless smile. "Carly, did I mention that you look pretty as a picture tonight?"

Carly froze. "Bill, if you think . . ."

He enveloped both her hands in his, his expression turning earnest. "Honey, there's not a man alive who'd be able to resist those big purple eyes of yours."

"Blue," she corrected absently. "And I think you'd better stop while we're still friends."

"Now, sugar, I'm not asking you to go to bed with the guy," he argued. "Just use a few of your feminine wiles and find out what Ryan is going to do."

"What if I discover he's going to gobble us up, like he did Houston Electronics?"

"Then you'll have to convince him to keep me on."

The amazing thing, Carly considered as she tugged firmly to retrieve her hands, was that Bill actually expected her to do it. Part of her felt compassion for the strong, decisive man he had been two years ago, before the accident. The other half was tempted to dump his drink over his head.

She had been struggling with the problem when Patrick Ryan had suddenly appeared at their table, shooting off the opening volley with his insinuating statement.

Now, as they waited for Bill McIntyre's return, a silence settled over the table—a verbal cease-fire—as each seemed to be waiting the other out.

"Look, Mr. Ryan," Carly said finally. "I don't know what Bill led you to expect, but I'm not one of the executive perks of Capitol Airlines."

"I never thought you were," Patrick replied smoothly.

Carly didn't quite trust his easy acquiescence. "Then why...?"

He folded his arms on the table, his mouth lifting a little at the corners as he watched her eyes fill with questions. They were beautiful eyes, Patrick considered. A deep, dark blue that was closer to violets than cornflowers, and fringed with lush, curly lashes that gleamed gold at the roots. As lovely as they admittedly were, Patrick found himself even more attracted by the intelligence he found in their depths.

From the way McIntyre had previously described Carly Ashton, dangling her in front of him like a ripe, juicy plum, Patrick had gotten the impression that the woman was nothing but a glorified mistress. One her partner was willing to share, if it would bolster his position with the man forced upon him by a concerned board of directors. After meeting Carly, Patrick was forced to alter that perception. Whatever her relationship with McIntyre, it would be beneficial to win her over to his side, if his plans for Capitol Airlines were to succeed. He had made a tactical error by allowing his distaste for McIntyre's unspoken offer to surface in his opening remark to Carly. That was unusual and for a brief moment Patrick wondered at his uncharacteristic behavior. He was not accustomed to making mistakes when it came to business dealings.

"You want to know why I acted like an ill-mannered oaf when I showed up at your table?"

She shrugged, tracing concentric circles on top of the table. A line formed between her brows as she considered his words.

"That's as good a description as any, I suppose," she replied. "Although my grandfather probably could have come up with quite a few far more colorful."

"He sounds a lot like my father. The senator would have me tarred and feathered for introducing myself to a lady that way."

Knowing Senator Michael Ryan, Carly laughed appreciatively. The man never shied away from calling things as he saw them, and the congressional record was peppered with nearly thirty years of his colorful quotes. But Carly had never heard the senator use anything stronger than a muttered "drat" in the presence of women. He flirted outrageously, but with an old-fashioned, chivalrous attitude that was as flattering as it was unthreatening.

"It would probably earn a trip to the woodshed," she agreed.

"You know my father?"

"Doesn't everyone? Administrations may come and go, but Mike Ryan is a Washington fixture. Like the Lincoln Memorial or the Smithsonian." She smiled. "He definitely proves that old adage about politics getting in your blood."

Patrick murmured a response that Carly didn't quite catch. She was about to ask him to repeat it when the maître d' returned with a message from Bill. Something unexpected had come up and he had been forced to leave.

"The old coward," she muttered. "He didn't even have the nerve to say goodbye."

"I don't blame him. You look mad enough to chew nails."

Carly glared at him. Then, as she viewed Bill's behavior from a different aspect, her exasperation dissolved.

"He didn't used to be like that," she said softly. Her fingertips rubbed wearily at her temples.

Patrick found himself wondering again about Carly's relationship with Bill McIntyre. Why had the man felt he could capitalize on her feminine appeal to ensure his own continued employment?

When Patrick didn't answer, Carly slowly lifted her head, her dark eyes trying to make him understand. "There was a time when the name Bill McIntyre guaranteed financial success. When everything he touched turned to gold." She managed a weak smile. "Or dividends."

Patrick nodded, disliking the intense loyalty he heard in her voice. That she cared about McIntyre very much was obvious. What he was suddenly determined to find out was the extent of her personal feelings.

Her fingernails glittered like rubies, and a small gold band on her right hand gleamed as it reflected the dining room light. Patrick couldn't forget the sight of those graceful hands clasped in McIntyre's burly paws.

"The past few years have been hard on him," she tried to explain without revealing too much of her friend's anguish.

Patrick's only response was an arched black brow. Carly thought she viewed a flicker of resentment in his eyes, but it was gone so quickly that she decided she must have imagined it.

"He's had personal problems," she elaborated.

"That's no excuse to run Capitol into the ground," Patrick pointed out. "If the guy can't cut it, he should get out and make room for those who can do the job right."

"Is that what you're going to do? Let him go?"

That had been the plan from the beginning, but Patrick was not ready to divulge his intentions. Instead of answering Carly's question, he gave her a lazy smile that usually worked wonders with women.

"Look, it's Friday night. The end of a long, grueling week for both of us. Since there'll be plenty of time to talk about business when the office opens on Monday, what do you say we forget about Capitol Airlines and enjoy a nice, leisurely meal?"

Carly didn't swoon at his feet, which didn't surprise him. Patrick had never met a woman less likely to swoon or capitulate without an argument. Her intelligent eyes met his coaxing gaze levelly.

"I have to warn you, if Capitol pays for this dinner and you take us over Monday morning, you'll probably be facing a bounced check charge."

"Are you always this candid?"

"Always. I've been described as unflinchingly honest."

"You make it sound like a character flaw."

"It seemed to be when I was working in public relations."

"And yet you had a very successful business going for yourself," Patrick pointed out.

Carly wasn't surprised the man had investigated her. "I had a number of important clients," she agreed. "But after a while I discovered I didn't want to spend the rest of my life creating smoke screens for profit."

"I never realized that was in the job description."

"Of course it is," Carly confirmed blithely. "But you've bought and sold enough companies to know how the game is played, Mr. Ryan. Industry manipulates people, grabs whatever it darn well wants, then goes out and hires a PR flack to make those actions appear noble."

"To an extent, I see your point," he surprised Carly by saying. "But I can't envision you as a flack."

"Neither could I. That's why I sold my business."

She plucked the olive from her glass, a smile of pleasure brightening her face as she enjoyed its tangy taste. "I don't care for martinis that much, but I do adore Spanish olives."

Patrick made a mental note to buy a case of Spanish olives at the first opportunity. "Is that when you went to work with McIntyre?"

Carly nodded. "That's right. Capitol was still a small commuter airline serving the Washington area when Bill offered me the position as vice president in charge of marketing and public relations. Since I was ready for a change, I sold my company and invested the money in Capitol. I still deal with people, but now I go to bed without a guilty conscience." Her level gaze met his. "Can you say the same, Mr. Ryan?" she challenged quietly.

She definitely had a knack for going straight to the heart of the matter, Patrick considered. "I sleep like a baby. Although there are those who'd suggest that's because I have no conscience."

Carly digested that for a moment. "Are they correct?"

"Why don't we leave that up to you to decide?"

"That sounds fair enough," Carly agreed. She smiled, but her dark blue eyes were sober. "I'm a very good judge of character, Mr. Ryan. My grandfather used to swear I had second sight."

"I'll take my chances," Patrick responded dryly. "And since we're going to be working closely together, why don't you call me Patrick?"

"I suppose I could manage that," she agreed. Her fingers began stroking the stem of her glass again.

Patrick stifled the errant sexual desire the gesture invoked and forced himself to remember what had brought him to Washington.

The scion of one of the country's most powerful political aristocracies, he had surprised everyone, including his father, when he'd eschewed politics for the financial world. Instead, after graduating from Columbia, followed by two years as a Rhodes scholar at Oxford, he had joined the Wall Street brokerage firm of Klein, Gotbaum and Albright as a financial consultant. There, after two long years number crunching, he had begun chafing under the restraints of a system that had been in effect for too many years to consider change.

Going out on his own, he had built a reputation for buying troubled companies, turning them around, then reselling them for a hefty profit. His detractors alleged that Patrick Ryan was ruthless, able to spot a struggling company the way a shark senses blood in the water. But early socialization went deep, and the Ryan family was renowned for its concern for the "common man." Patrick began to find it more and more difficult to capitalize on the misfortune of others.

It was then he had become interested in what was being referred to in the marketplace as "worker capitalism." Instead of buying the foundering lumber mill in southern Oregon, he created a deal whereby the workers purchased half interest in the mill in exchange for a reduction in wages. As part owners, the employees played a role in the boardroom as well as in the mill, gaining a say in choosing equipment and devising ways to increase productivity. It proved inordinately successful. The workers' jobs were saved while management kept its company. Patrick's position was one of consultant; he worked strictly on a fee basis.

Although it represented a radical break from corporate tradition, Patrick accomplished the same feat three more times before being approached by Bill McIntyre and the board of Capitol Airlines. During a series of secret meetings, they had given Patrick carte blanche in the hopes that he would be able to perform similar magic on their own struggling company. Not that they had any choice, he considered, remembering the heated tone of some of those meetings.

A few more vocal board members had accused him of using the opportunity to manipulate his own takeover. Patrick had the distinct impression that had Carly been at any of those meetings, she would have been in his opponents' corner.

He had prevailed, as expected. An agreement was reached that during reorganization, Bill McIntyre would take a leave of absence. The announcement would be made Monday morning.

Despite his ability to walk the narrow tightrope between financial success and his family's liberal ideals, Patrick was still first and foremost a businessman. Every instinct he possessed told him that in order to achieve results, Bill McIntyre would have to go. Permanently. Realizing how Carly would react, Patrick chose to keep that little detail to himself for now.

The conversation remained casual as they discussed the unseasonably cold weather, the Redskins' last appearance in the Super Bowl, and the recent developments in the Middle East. Carly, he noted with interest, approached each topic with enthusiasm, her hands fluttering gracefully in the air to emphasize her words. They were a dancer's hands, he decided. Or those of a pianist.

They had finished dinner and were lingering over coffee when two men stopped by the table on their way out of the restaurant.

The tall blonde greeted her with unrestrained warmth. "Carly! You look terrific, as usual."

She lowered her cup to the table and rose, giving the man a warm, unselfconscious hug. "My God," she said with a laugh, "so it's true. The inmates are actually running the asylum."

"Is that any way to talk to your Chief of State's newest speech writer?"

"Excuse me, your excellency," Carly apologized, dipping into a low curtsy. As she looked past the writer to his companion, her eyes sparkled with affection.

"Alex," she greeted the darker of the two men, "what on earth are you doing with this renegade?"

Alexander Bedare bestowed a light kiss on Carly's cheek. "You know I never overlook an opportunity to make new acquaintances," he answered smoothly. "Although it's always wonderful to see old friends. Especially the beautiful ones."

Belatedly remembering her manners, Carly turned to Patrick. "I'd like you to meet a couple of my more silver-tongued friends. Brent Daniels is the administration's newest golden-haired boy. I'm sure you've read his stuff. Brent was with the *New York Times* for years and years."

"Not that many years," Brent protested laughingly. "You make me sound like the Ancient Mariner."

Carly dismissed his complaint. "Oh, pooh, you were obviously a child prodigy." She continued her introductions. "Alexander Bedare," she said, nodding toward the dark-haired man, "is attached to the Egyptian embassy. Fellows, this is Patrick Ryan."

With the attitude of a quintessential reporter used to cultivating sources in high places, Brent shifted his attention immediately from Carly to Patrick.

"It's a distinct pleasure to meet you," he stated, extending his hand. "I've always admired your father."

"Doesn't everyone," Patrick responded dryly. He rose to shake Brent's hand, then smiled at the Egyptian diplomat. "Alex, you old camel trader, I planned on looking you up tomorrow. How are things going?"

"Same as always," Alex replied with an expansive shrug. "We make a little ground, lose some, then gain it back again. But you know how it goes in the world of international politics."

"Only too well," Patrick agreed.

Carly thought she detected a bit of sarcasm in Patrick's tone, but her surprise that the two men were acquainted kept her from dwelling on its possible cause.

"You know each other?"

Alex's broad smile flashed white under his black mustache. "We went to school together; Patrick is responsible for all my vices."

"I see you're still as much of a liar as you ever were," Patrick countered with an answering grin. Carly couldn't help noticing how the genuine warmth altered his features, softening the rugged planes of his face. "You're a natural for the diplomatic service."

"Or the business world," Alex retorted. "Watch this guy, Carly. He has a way of making up his own rules."

Carly's appraising gaze settled on Patrick. "I've figured that much out for myself."

Patrick didn't like the way his old friend's arm had settled so naturally around her waist, although why it should bother him, he didn't understand. Nevertheless, he didn't like it. Not one bit.

He dragged his gaze away from the dark hand splayed on Carly's silk-covered hip. "I'm surprised you two know each other."

"Carly introduced me to American jazz. She assured me that I couldn't pass myself off as an expert on this great country of yours if I couldn't appreciate its native music."

Patrick was not surprised Carly was a jazz aficionada; he'd already determined there was a complex individual lurking underneath that attractive packaging. He wondered idly what had happened to all Alex's country and western albums. Alex had been fascinated by the American West when they'd first met and was the only person Patrick knew who not only possessed every record Buck Owens ever cut, but had a vintage souvenir album dedicated to the cowboys of the Calgary Stampede as well.

"Speaking of which," Carly broke in, looking up at Alex, "two tickets to Tuesday night's Mangione concert fell into my hands today. How would you like to go with me?"

Alex's answering smile could have melted all the snow accumulating on the sidewalk outside the bustling restaurant. "Are you kidding? Who did you have to kill for those? That concert's been sold out for weeks."

Carly laughed. "Let's just say that you're not the only one who can use diplomacy to your own advantage," she said. "Well, is it a date?"

"Not only is it a date, I'll even spring for dinner," Alex promised expansively.

Carly gave a mock sigh and fluttered her lashes in a flirtatious manner Scarlett O'Hara would have envied. "The last of the big spenders," she drawled. "Just think how nice it would be if you had some of all that lovely oil money. We could go first class."

Alex patted her cheek. "For Mangione, we go first class."

For Carly, who'd been living exclusively on macaroni and cheese these days, trying to draw as little as possible from Capitol Airlines, the prospect of an expensive meal, topped off by two hours of Chuck Mangione's magnificent flügelhorn, was pure nirvana.

"You're on," she agreed instantly.

After they had finished making plans, the two men departed the restaurant, leaving Carly and Patrick alone once again.

"Alex is a nice man," Carly said, taking a sip of the now cooled coffee.

Patrick mumbled an inarticulate reply, scribbled his name at the bottom of the credit card receipt lying on the small plastic tray, then placed his napkin on the table in a decisive gesture.

"Ready to go?"

At Patrick's brusque tone, Carly glanced up at him in surprise. They'd managed to get along fine during dinner, once they had put away the antagonism that had sparked from his first uncomplimentary statement. So what was his problem now? Unwilling to worry about the cause of Patrick Ryan's ill temper, Carly decided it was definitely time to call it a night.

"I think we'd better," she agreed, glancing over at the maître d'. "Nick has been eyeing this table for the past ten minutes." She rose, picking up her purse. "Thank you for dinner. I'll see you Monday morning."

Despite his lingering irritation at the way Carly seemed so generous with her affections, Patrick wasn't quite ready to let her get away.

"I'll drop you off at your place," he announced abruptly. He plucked her coat from the vacant chair.

As Carly slipped her arms into the sleeves, she stifled her aggravation that Patrick seemed to be giving her little choice in the matter. "You needn't bother."

"It isn't any bother." His hands rested lightly, but unmistakably possessively, on her shoulders.

Shrugging free of his touch, Carly held her ground. "That's very nice of you, but I have my own car."

"That's even better." He met the flash of irritation sparking her dark blue eyes with a bland expression of his own. "You can drop me off on your way home and save me taxi fare."

They exchanged a long, somewhat challenging look, both aware that the cease-fire was over, the battle resumed anew. Reminding herself that she would be wise to save her energy for the fight that was bound to begin Monday morning, Carly merely lifted one slender shoulder in an uncaring shrug.

"Far be it for me not to offer you a little of our Southern hospitality," she stated with a distinct lack of enthusiasm.

Resting his broad hand lightly on the back of her wool coat, Patrick allowed himself a victorious smile. "That's precisely what I was hoping you'd say."

Ignoring the invitation in his tone, as well as the warmth of his fingers splayed against her back, Carly walked stiffly from the restaurant.

She would simply drive him to the hotel, then drop him off at the door, she assured herself. If he thought he was getting her up to his room, he could just think again. Because if there was one thing she'd already discerned from her initial contact with Patrick Ryan, it was that the man was much too used to getting his own way.

If he harbored any notions that she was going to fall into his arms, or his bed for that matter, he was sadly mistaken. She didn't particularly like the man, Carly reminded herself firmly as they made their way through the throng of congressmen waiting in the lobby for a free table. And even if she did, she would never condone what he was planning to do to Bill.

Loyalty was one of Carly's strongest traits; she would never sell out a friend. Not for money, power, prestige or because the enemy had a way of making her all too aware of the innate differences between a man and a woman.

2

THE FOLLOWING MORNING Patrick found, to his increasing irritation, that twelve hours had done nothing to lessen his desire for, or his fascination with, Carly Ashton.

She was too tall, Patrick had reminded himself all night. His tastes ran more to petite women, women who had to tilt their heads back enchantingly to look up at him, their gazes adoring and seductive. Carly's pansy-blue eyes, on the other hand, had met his levelly, issuing a continual series of challenges. She was too skinny. He preferred soft curves in his bed, not boyish angles. The usual women of his acquaintance were complaisant, their only wish to please him. Carly was going to fight him tooth and nail on the Capitol deal. Patrick knew it.

She wasn't his type. So why couldn't he get her out of his mind?

Deciding that sitting around brooding about the woman was definitely not constructive behavior, Patrick picked up the telephone and arranged a racquetball game with Alex for early that afternoon.

STILL UNABLE TO DISMISS Carly from his thoughts, Patrick tried to drive her out of his mind as he raced back and forth across the racquetball court, taking out his frustration on the hard rubber ball.

"My point," Alex called out as the well-placed shot slid down a wall. "I win. Two games to one," he announced happily.

"You bandit," Patrick muttered. "You never used to be able to return my serves that well."

"That was many years ago, my friend," Alex replied. "Things have changed."

"That's for sure," Patrick agreed grimly, his mind going back to those seemingly carefree days of their youth.

He had met Alexander Bedare his first day in England, the Rhodes scholar from Massachusetts and the young Egyptian far from home finding a common bond in the strange atmosphere of Oxford University. They shared a flat for over a year, until Patrick's marriage. Even when the twosome turned into a threesome, they had remained steadfast friends. Alex had been the best man at Patrick and Julia's wedding. Although their lives had taken separate paths after Oxford, they kept in touch, corresponding regularly. When Alex had arrived in New York as part of the Egyptian delegation to the United Nations, he and Patrick slipped easily and naturally into their old relationship.

Alex proved to be a pillar of strength during those long months of Julia's illness, standing by as she fought the valiant, but futile battle with leukemia. And he had stood beside Patrick in the icy winter rain, watching as the simple coffin was lowered into the frozen ground. Shortly after Julia's death, Alex had accepted an assignment in Washington.

Julia had loved Alex openly and warmly, yet that fact had never disturbed Patrick. He had never experienced that unwelcome surge of jealousy the sight of his old friend's hand resting so comfortably on the soft swell of Carly Ashton's hip had invoked last night. On the contrary, Patrick considered, thinking back as he stood under the shower in the club locker room, it would have been difficult if his wife hadn't loved

Alex. The ebullient Egyptian had been an integral part of his life in those days, and he would not have wanted to choose between his best friend and the lovely young woman he had married.

But the problem never arose. Julia had unabashedly adored Patrick; she accepted everything and everyone in his life. In addition to such unqualified love, she had brought him peace and harmony. And support when he needed it most to survive his family's dissatisfaction with his career goals. In some respects, Julia and Alex had generated more feelings of family than he'd ever felt growing up in his father's household.

As Patrick dressed in his street clothes, he shook off the melancholy thoughts, assuring himself that it was only seeing his old friend again that had stimulated such feelings of loneliness. He continued to tell himself that as he and Alex settled down over a pitcher of beer.

"Ah, America," Alex said, sighing happily. "I much prefer your cold beer to what we used to drink." He wiped the foam from his mouth with the back of his hand.

"I don't remember you ever turning down the warm stuff," Patrick stated. "We had some good times, didn't we?"

"We did indeed," Alex agreed with a smile. "By the way, I've heard rumors that your father is actually going to retire at the end of his current term. Is this true?"

"That's what he says, although I wouldn't bet the farm on it. I can't see Dad spending his afternoons playing golf or puttering around in a workshop. And he's a lousy fisherman." Patrick gave Alex a grim smile. "Besides, how would the people of Massachusetts survive without a Ryan representing them in the Senate?"

"There's also a persistent story making the rounds that another Ryan will be taking up the political banner," Alex answered. "Is that why you're visiting our fair city? Have you given further consideration to your father's master plan?"

Patrick lowered his mug to the table with more force than necessary. "Tell me the truth—can you see me as a politician?"

Instead of laughing, as Patrick suspected his friend might, Alex surveyed him silently, his dark eyes sober as he considered the question.

"No," he said finally. "The machine might be able to win the election for you, but you'd never last in this town. You're too intransigent and far too honest to be a successful politician."

"You don't believe an honest man can survive in Washington?" Patrick asked with interest.

"Do you? *Mr. Smith Goes to Washington* was a delightful movie, Patrick. I watch it whenever it's on the late show. But Jimmy Stewart wouldn't survive five minutes in today's political arena."

His eyes flicked judiciously over Patrick. "In fact, on second thought, I take back my words about the Ryan machine winning the election for you. Voters need to feel close to the men they elect; they want to shake their hands, hold up chubby, rosy-cheeked babies to be kissed. The electorate is intimidated by men who entrench themselves behind walls of ice."

How many times had Julia said the same thing to him, during those difficult days when he had been estranged from his parents, Patrick wondered. That was one of the reasons he had loved her. And it was why he'd also loved this ebullient Egyptian. Both could always be counted on to tell him the truth, not what they thought he might want to hear.

"That sounds vaguely familiar."

"You still miss her." Alex's dark eyes were sympathetic.

Patrick sighed. "I don't know.... I've gotten over her death," he answered slowly. "But there are times when I miss having someone to share my life with." He attempted a smile that didn't quite succeed. "It gets damn lonely at the top," he said, his intended jest falling flat.

"You should be married," Alex declared. "It's been five years, Patrick. It's time to put those days behind you and get on with your life."

"I've put those days behind me," Patrick responded a bit too harshly. Lowering his voice, he picked up the mug, staring into the amber depths of dark beer. "But I have no intention of ever getting married again."

His tone did not encourage an argument and Alex wisely refrained from continuing the conversation along that line. Instead, he turned the topic to last night.

"So if you are not in Washington for political reasons, perhaps it has to do with our lovely Miss Ashton?"

Patrick's head jerked up and he speared Alex with a particularly sharp gaze. "My relationship with Carly Ashton is merely business."

Alex's smile was smooth, innocent and, Patrick determined, entirely false. "That's the type of business a man could find himself enjoying very much. No wonder you rejected politics for the corporate arena."

"How long have you known her?"

Alex didn't hesitate. "About five years. She was one of the first people I met when I moved here."

"How did you meet her?"

Alex's dark eyes seemed to be appraising Patrick thoughtfully, but his tone remained casual. "The same way you meet everyone in this town. At a party." His brow furrowed. "I believe she was dating an undersecretary of state at the time.... That's right. The guy was what you call in this country a hunk. Tall, wavy hair, disgustingly flat stomach. He could probably have his own television show if he ever gave up foreign service."

Patrick found himself hating the man without even knowing his name. "He seems to have made quite an impression."

"They made quite an attractive couple," Alex admitted. "I remember thinking they looked as if they belonged on the top of a wedding cake. The man was obviously head over heels in love with her, but aren't we all," he added with an ironical smile. "When she spent half the evening talking music with me, I thought I'd discovered heaven on earth."

"She seems to like you."

Alex's eyes narrowed at Patrick's gritty tone. "We're friends, Patrick. Nothing more." He sighed heavily. "Not that I wouldn't like a more intimate relationship with the lovely Carly. But I care about her too much to take the chance of losing her friendship."

"What do you mean by that?"

"You know how the women outnumber the men in Washington."

Patrick nodded.

"I enjoy those numbers. I find them suitable to an unencumbered social life."

"Still into hit-and-run relationships, I see."

"You were always the one with a distressing tendency toward monogamy," Alex observed with a crooked smile.

Patrick's eyes turned hard as he gave his friend a silent warning. "As you pointed out, those days are far behind us."

While Alex looked inclined to argue, he merely shook his head. "Carly is a nice woman, Patrick. She deserves better."

The tables were suddenly turned as Patrick detected a warning in Alex's smooth tones. His chair legs scraped against the floor as he rose abruptly.

"Thanks for the game. Next time I'll be better prepared."

"Next time," Alex murmured, rising as well. He embraced Patrick, his eyes sparkling, as if he knew a secret he was not

prepared to reveal. "I wish you luck with your business dealings, my friend."

Patrick eyed him carefully, seeking a sign of double meaning in his tone. But because he was always the diplomat,
Alex's answering gaze was smooth, his smile guileless.

"Thanks," Patrick muttered. "I'll call you next week and
we'll do the town."

"Any evening but Tuesday," he agreed cheerfully.

The Mangione concert, Patrick remembered. The one Alex
was attending with Carly. Suddenly he wanted to get out of
the smoke-filled bar and into the fresh air, where he could
clear his head.

"Have fun at your concert," he threw back over his shoulder as he strode purposefully toward the door.

Alex merely nodded, watching with interest as Patrick
jammed his hands into his pockets and walked out into the
cold.

PATRICK WAS NOT the only one feeling unsettled after last
night's meeting. Carly had spent most of the day casting wary
glances in the direction of the silent telephone, half expecting Patrick to call.

He had done a valiant job of hiding his annoyance when
she'd refused his invitation to join him for an afterdinner
drink at the hotel, but it was clear he had expected her to ac-
quiesce. They had fought another battle of wills, and though
Carly had emerged the victor in the renewed skirmish, she
was not foolish enough to think she'd won the war.

She tried to lose herself in a recent bestseller, only to find
that she had read the first page at least ten times without remembering a single word. Tossing the book aside, she spent
the next hour throwing paint at a canvas she'd prepared last
weekend. But her heart wasn't in her work and, standing back

to view her creation, Carly decided that all she had managed to do was waste expensive paint and ruin a fresh canvas.

Determined to expunge the man from her mind, she sat down at the piano, her fingers punishing the keys as if she imagined them to be Patrick Ryan. What was it about him that had her so disconcerted? It wasn't his thinly veiled seduction attempts; Carly would have been able to handle them with her usual skill and diplomacy.

She was not unaware of the fact that she was an attractive woman. Perhaps not as beautiful as her mother, or at least the pictures she'd seen of Bettina Ashton. But her features were put together in a pleasing enough manner and she'd never lacked for admirers. While her slender figure tended toward angles rather than the voluptuous curves she would have preferred, her small breasts were firm and her long legs were well shaped, thanks in part to her weekly dance classes.

Her natural good looks, plus an enthusiasm for life and a sense of humor handed down by her grandfather, had earned Carly a handful of proposals over the years. Yet despite her desire for a home and family, she consistently turned down those offers, displaying a romantic streak she did her best to keep hidden from public view.

It was not that she suffered from a Cinderella complex, Carly considered now, her fingers moving fluidly, automatically, over the keys. She wasn't waiting breathlessly for a handsome prince to come riding up on a white charger and carry her off to his palace. Yet she was waiting for... something, she admitted, her hands dropping into her lap as she contemplated the matter.

She had made a success of her life. She might not be outrageously wealthy, or powerful, which was an even better barometer of success in Washington, but she had carved a niche for herself that was comfortable as well as satisfying. She enjoyed her work, even as hectic as things had been around the office the past few mònths. She had a number of friends and experienced an active and fulfilling social life. So why was she feeling at such loose ends today?

Heaving a frustrated sigh, she gave up on the intricate Bach movement and pulled a purple, fleece-lined jacket from a brass coatrack in the corner. Since the light snow from last night had turned to exhaust-blackened slush, she tugged on a pair of high leather boots, as well. A wool cap and pair of gloves and she was prepared to walk off her restlessness.

The wind tugged at her jacket and blew her hair into a mass of tangles as Carly walked the nearly deserted streets of downtown Washington. She stopped for a time in a small café, warming herself with a cup of hot chocolate. The waitress seemed inclined toward conversation, but Carly was not in the mood for idle chitchat. After agreeing that the lousy weather was probably keeping everyone indoors, she fell silent, finishing her drink before resuming her solitary walk.

"If I had an ounce of sense," Carly muttered as she cut across the brown lawn of Lafayette Park, "I'd be at home, in front of a warm fire right now. Instead of wandering the streets like a bag lady."

Bending forward against the stiff winter breeze, Carly imagined the fragrant scent of cedar logs, the crackling flames sending their warmth throughout her modest apartment. Attempting to banish the chill, she willed herself to envision the red and orange flames, to feel the heat.

Unfortunately the mental exercise worked too well; the image conjured up another vision far more warmth inspiring, far too provoking. Unbidden, Patrick Ryan appeared in her mind's eye, lounging casually on the braided rag rug in front of her hearth, his crystal-blue eyes reflecting the brilliant gleam of the firelight. One of her grandfather's women friends had described those eyes once while mooning over an old Robert Mitchum movie on television. Bedroom eyes, she'd called them. As Carly imagined herself pulled into their swirling depths, she decided the term definitely fitted.

A harsh gust of wind rattled the branches of a tree overhead, snapping her from her intimate reverie. "Damn," she muttered, jamming her hands into her jacket pockets, "this has to stop. You can't negotiate with the man on Monday morning if you keep getting all mushy whenever you think of him!"

Spinning on her heel, she marched out of the park, headed to the warmth of her apartment. The wind stung her cheeks and though she felt chilled all the way to the bone, Carly welcomed the discomfort. It kept her unruly mind from creating erotic images of Patrick Ryan.

Her resolve melted away as she found him waiting outside her building. Fighting down the surge of joy his unexpected appearance created, she forced herself to walk slowly toward him.

"This is a surprise." Carly rewarded herself on maintaining an aura of reasonable curiosity, but no outward interest in the man himself.

"Believe me, it's as much a surprise to me as it is to you," Patrick answered. "I'm not in the habit of shivering in doorways waiting for a woman who's already decided I'm the enemy."

That he was perceptive did not surprise Carly. He would have to possess that trait to be as successful as he was. What did surprise her, however, was his candor.

"Aren't you?" she challenged.

"I'm not wearing a black hat, Carly."

Actually, Carly noted belatedly, he wasn't wearing any hat. His thick black curls were windblown, his face ruddy with the cold. The tips of his ears were bright red.

"How long have you been standing out here?"

"About an hour."

Her eyes widened. "You must be freezing."

Patrick shook his head. "I think I passed that state twenty minutes ago." His teeth began to clack together as he attempted a smile.

"Well, we'll have to do something about warming you up," Carly stated briskly, taking his arm as she unlocked the outer door of the building.

"I'm all for that," he agreed amiably.

"Don't get any wrong ideas," she warned as they entered the small cage of the elevator. "I'm only doing this for Capitol Airlines. Since you seem to be all we having going for us right now, it'd be a shame to let you die of pneumonia."

As the ancient elevator rose, its cable creaking ominously, Carly was unable to miss the shivers Patrick was trying hard to suppress.

"I think I like the idea of being your white knight."

She couldn't help laughing at that description. "I think you're far from that, Patrick. But it's still no reason to let you freeze to death in my doorway."

"Thank you. I had resigned myself to becoming one more statue for the pigeons to abuse."

"I wouldn't have wanted that to happen."

"Really?"

"Of course not," she replied blithely as the elevator opened onto her floor. "There are far too many statues in Washington already."

Patrick chuckled appreciatively as he followed her into her apartment.

"Give me your coat, then sit down on the couch," she instructed with a wave of her hand. "I'll get some brandy and start a fire."

"Ah, Carly." He sighed with pleasure as he handed over his stiff wool topcoat and settled down on the overstuffed couch.

"I knew that deep within that prickly exterior there dwelt the heart of an angel."

Carly didn't answer as she left the room, but his huskily stated words stirred something deep within her. What was it about Patrick Ryan that could make her feel like Napoleon facing down Wellington at Waterloo, then without a blink of his eyes, stimulated feelings more appropriate to Eve facing her mate in the Garden?

Unable to come up with an answer, she filled a copper kettle and put it on for tea. Locating the brandy, she put the bottle on a tray with two snifters. On an afterthought, she pulled a box of Girl Scout cookies from the cupboard. Her grandfather had taught her to always offer food to a guest, and though Patrick didn't exactly qualify as such—she certainly hadn't invited him here—early socialization went deep. She'd allow him to warm up, then she'd feed him. And then, before she gave into impulses better left in check, she'd send him on his way.

Patrick took advantage of Carly's absence to roam the room, studying the eclectic mix of furniture that, while unfashionable in the days of pastel colors and art deco furnishings, suited her perfectly. The overstuffed sofa was covered in a bright floral fabric, and the cushions tied to the maple rocker boasted vibrant stripes. She'd painted the walls white, the high ceiling a light blue. With the vast array of plants adorning every flat surface, she had created an atmosphere of perpetual springtime. All in all, he decided, the room was as vivid and unpretentious as its owner.

An easel stood in the corner, the canvas splashed with bright, primary colors that made up for the lack of sunshine outside the window. A needlepoint canvas lay on the seat of a flower-sprigged wing chair, displaying a partially stitched orange cat. Tangled yarn scattered atop a nearby side table revealed the impatience that kept her from taking the time to sort the strands by color, as was his mother's habit when doing needlework.

Patrick leafed through the stack of sheet music on top of the old upright piano, finding everything from Beethoven to the Beatles, Mangione to Manilow. Her taste in music, it appeared, was as eclectic and unpredictable as the lady herself. His gaze circled the room, settling on a pair of black shoes, tied with bright red ribbons. Closer examination revealed metal toes and heels.

"You tap-dance," he stated, looking back over his shoulder as Carly returned.

Observing the shiny patent leather shoe in his hand, Carly wished, not for the first time, that she could bring the same sense of organization she displayed in her professional life to her personal one. If she'd put those shoes away in the closet where they belonged, she'd never have to admit to such a frivolous pastime in front of the one man she needed to impress with her business sense.

"It's an excellent aerobic exercise. Here, I brought you a drink." Patrick had already started the fire. Its bright blaze sent a warmth to all four corners of the room.

Patrick caught the slight edge of defensiveness in Carly's tone and sought to dispel any misconception she might be harboring. Their relationship was going to be difficult enough come Monday morning. He didn't want to sabotage it with misunderstandings that had nothing to do with his interest in her airline.

"I love tap dancers. In fact, I've sat through old Shirley Temple movies just for the pleasure of watching Bill Bojangles Robinson and I'm a regular at Radio City Music Hall." He gave Carly a boyishly attractive smile. "I'm a sucker for the Rockettes."

"I'll bet," Carly murmured, picturing the leggy dancers.

"Hey, really," Patrick protested. "When I was a kid, I tried to talk my parents into letting me take lessons, but the senator insisted I play football instead. He said tap-dancing was for sissies."

As he heard himself saying the words, Patrick wondered what it was about this woman that had him revealing something so personal. He never talked about his childhood. Not even to Alex or Julia, who had known him more intimately than anyone.

"Try telling that to Gene Kelly," Carly suggested dryly.

Patrick surprised them both by laughing, a deep, full-bodied sound. "That's the same thing I said."

Deciding that he might not be teasing her after all, Carly relented, handing him the brandy. "You're still ice cold," she protested as their hands brushed.

"But warming up fast."

Carly found herself drowning in his clear blue eyes and suddenly this scene was all too reminiscent of her sensual fantasy. She sought something to say, anything that might break the silken web settling over them.

"He and my grandfather were close friends."

Patrick's gaze settled on her lips. "Who?" he murmured absently.

Carly found herself unable to answer and swallowed deeply, forcing her mind to carry on the casual conversation.

"Bill Robinson," she managed finally.

"You're kidding!"

She shook her head, wondering what on earth had possessed her to tell him that. It wasn't that she was embarrassed or ashamed of her grandfather. He'd given her a great deal of love, and had been the rock on which the foundation of their small family had been built. But his colorful career, not to mention his unorthodox cronies, did not constitute the businesslike persona Carly felt she should be displaying for Patrick Ryan while he held her future in his hands.

"No. Gramps was a headliner on the old vaudeville circuit," she allowed.

"What did he do when vaudeville died?"

"He tried movies, but it didn't work out, so like a lot of out-of-work performers, he moved to burlesque. Since the shows were admittedly risqué, there was always one act on the bill designed to keep the police from closing down the theaters." Carly smiled faintly. "My grandfather was that act."

She picked up the yarn from the table, absently tangling the bright strands of wool even more with nervous fingers as she wondered how much to tell him. Carly surprised herself by continuing the story.

"My mother ran off with a musician and when I was born, she brought me home for Gramps to raise. He decided burlesque wasn't the best atmosphere for a child and found other work."

Deciding that she had already revealed too much, Carly put down the yarn. "Really, Patrick, you can't possibly be that interested in all this."

"Of course I am."

She stuck her hands in her pockets and stared at the fire. "I find that difficult to believe, after the exciting life you've led."

Patrick shrugged. "My life was extremely uneventful, Carly. All I remember is a continual parade of housekeepers until I was old enough to go to military school." His tone softened encouragingly. "Tell me about your grandfather. I want to know all about him."

"Why?"

"Because I think there's a great deal of him in you," Patrick answered simply. "And I want to know everything about you."

The husky note in his voice did nothing to instill calm. "Why?" she repeated.

"I don't know," he admitted. "But when I figure it out, I promise to let you know." He gave her a coaxing half smile. "Carry on, Carly. I'm fascinated."

Giving up on solving the puzzle for now, Carly decided that her past was not really a secret. With all his resources, Patrick Ryan could learn anything about anyone. What could it hurt?

"My grandfather was—" she sought an appropriate word "—colorful. If he'd been rich, he probably would have been described as eccentric. Since he wasn't, a lot of people called him crazy. . . . He danced a little, sang a little less and told horrible old jokes. But he was a dynamite magician. We settled in Florida and he played the Jacksonville clubs and anywhere else he could get work. Moose lodges, Elks, VFW, we played them all."

"We?"

She smiled reminiscently. "I was seven when he put me in the act."

"Doing what?"

"*I* didn't do anything. He cut me in half."

She still had her back to him and Patrick crossed the room to stand behind her. "I'm relieved that he managed to put all the pieces back in all the right places," he murmured, his lips near her ear. "They're very enticing pieces."

Carly slowly turned to face him. "Patrick," she said hesitantly, "Please don't do this."

"I can't help myself." He studied her thoughtfully. Carly was relieved when he suddenly seemed to change the subject. "Did he teach you any of his tricks?"

"As a matter of fact, he did. I love magic; I do benefit performances around town whenever I get a chance."

"That may just explain it."

"Explain what?"

"It's obvious that you inherited your grandfather's talent, Carly. Is it magic that makes me so attracted to you, I wonder?"

Carly turned away. "I don't want to talk about this," she insisted.

"Do you want me to leave?"

No, Carly considered weakly. She didn't really want him to go. She just didn't want him to be continually sparking these confusing feelings. She needed time to sort everything out.

"Would you like to see his scrapbooks?" she asked suddenly.

Although it wasn't his first choice, Patrick agreed and Carly went into the bedroom, dragging out the stacks of aged paper encased in leather bindings. Leaving him the scrapbooks, she went into the kitchen to prepare the tea.

Two hours later, the teapot was empty and all that remained of the cookies were a few scattered crumbs on the plate. The time had flown as they'd sat in front of the fire, looking through the albums together. It certainly hadn't been the way she'd pictured them spending time with each other, but the afternoon had been undeniably enjoyable.

"I suppose he taught you to dance," Patrick guessed.

Carly nodded. "He did, though he always said I inherited any musical talent I have from my parents. My mother was a singer and my father played the saxophone."

Patrick's eyes swept over the vibrant canvases covering the high white walls. "You're a woman of many talents."

"It was my great-grandmother who was the artist," Carly amazed herself by revealing. "She was quite a bohemian."

"You realize, of course, that you've piqued my interest again," Patrick drawled as Carly fell silent. "You can't just leave a statement like that dangling without elaborating."

Carly wondered if a man from Patrick's illustrious family tree could possibly appreciate her admittedly unorthodox roots. Probably not. She decided that the safest thing to do would be to point out all their differences in the beginning. Before she found herself becoming involved with him.

"Her name was Maggie Ashton and she lived in Greenwich Village back when it was still a village. It was becoming a mecca for artists and she had a patron—a married city councilman—who broke off their relationship because of political pressures."

"And he was your great-grandfather?"

"No, my great-grandfather was a banker. They met when he came to evict her. After the councilman left her, her painting income wasn't nearly enough to pay the rent."

Carly grinned. "According to Gramps, she never let a little thing like money stand in the way of happiness. Anyway, that staid banker had never met anyone with such a zest for living. The poor guy didn't stand a chance. They say it was love at first sight." She held out her right hand, displaying a slender gold band. "This was her wedding ring."

Patrick could sympathize with the love-struck banker and asked the question that came immediately to mind. "Do you by any chance look like your great-grandmother?"

"Gramps always said I did." Carly flipped through the album, locating a photograph of Maggie Ashton. "What do you think?"

Patrick studied the faded sepia photo. The lower half of the blond woman's face was hidden by a black lace fan. But he'd recognize those eyes anywhere.

"I think," he said slowly, lifting his gaze to Carly, "that I can understand precisely how your great-grandfather felt."

More than a little flustered by the warmth gleaming in Patrick's eyes, Carly turned her attention to the scrapbook, her fingers trembling slightly as she turned the page to a newspaper photo of Sally Rand, precariously covered by her famous fans. Patrick's gaze moved from the faded clipping to skim over Carly's slender curves.

"I don't suppose you learned anything else from all this exposure to the theatrical world?" he asked hopefully.

Guessing what was running through his mind, Carly allowed a small, enticing smile. "A few things."

"Would you be willing to give me a demonstration?"

Carly spent the next five minutes demurring with feminine reluctance while Patrick continued to wheedle like a small boy requesting a shiny red bicycle from Santa Claus. Finally she capitulated, insisting Patrick remain where he was while she got ready. When she returned, still clad in the bulky red sweater and jeans, he lifted an inquiring brow.

There was a moment of stunned silence, then Patrick burst into deep, appreciative laughter as she began expertly juggling three oranges, an apple and a banana.

He rose from the braided rug. "I like your style, Carly Ashton."

All conscious thought scattered to the winds as he held out his arms, inviting Carly into his embrace. Fruit fell unheeded to the floor as she moved slowly toward him, unable to resist the silent appeal.

At the touch of Patrick's wide hands against her back, Carly sighed, her own arms going around his waist as she rested her forehead against the firm line of his shoulder. While she knew she was being incredibly fanciful, she couldn't help thinking that she had never experienced anything quite so satisfying as simply standing here in Patrick's arms.

"Ah, Carly," he murmured, pushing aside her hair, allowing his lips access to her throat. "You're making it extremely difficult for me to behave in proper knightly fashion."

She lifted her head. "I thought we'd determined that you're a far cry from a white knight."

Patrick failed to smile at her soft jest. "Chivalry definitely was the furthest thing from my mind when I came here today."

Carly couldn't resist running her fingers through those enticing black curls, finding them as silky as they'd been in her fantasy. As the gesture fitted her body more closely to his, Patrick's hands slid down her back.

They fitted together perfectly—chest to breast, thigh to thigh—the warmth of his body communicating itself to her even through the heavy barrier of winter clothing.

"I never did ask why you came here today," Carly remembered, even as she succumbed to the enticing heat.

"The reason should be obvious, Carly," Patrick stated calmly. "I came here to make love to you."

3

STUNNED BY HIS CANDOR, as well as his gritty, unromantic tone, Carly dropped her hands to her sides. "Didn't you take into consideration the fact that I might not want to go to bed with you?"

"I considered that."

"And?"

Patrick smiled, but there was no warmth in it. His eyes remained unnervingly cool. "I came to the conclusion that you didn't get any more sleep last night than I did. The logical solution was for us to get the sexual part of our relationship out of the way before we have to get down to business on Monday morning."

Carly backed away, noticing that Patrick did nothing to stop her. But she could feel his unwavering gaze on her as she walked on unsteady legs to the window.

Mrs. McGregor was walking her dogs, Carly noted absently, as the elderly woman did everyday, rain or shine, summer or winter. The sight of the three dachshunds waddling down the sidewalk, the equally overweight woman trailing behind, trying to keep the leashes from becoming tangled, usually made Carly smile. But not today.

"Are you always this casual about your relationships?" she asked finally, as the pudgy quartet disappeared around the corner.

Patrick remained where he was, waiting patiently, his hands deep in the pockets of his slacks. "Always," he said simply, knowing that was not entirely the truth.

There had been nothing casual in his relationship with Julia. But that had been a very long time ago. To Patrick it seemed like another lifetime.

It was ironic, Carly thought as his answer sank in. She had never been unduly disturbed by the fact that she wasn't constantly falling in love, like Marge, her secretary, or Heather, who rattled on about a new heartthrob at each week's dancing class. Instead of worrying about what she didn't have, Carly had always concentrated on what she did have. Her work. And her friends.

Then Patrick Ryan appeared from out of the blue and before twenty-four hours had passed, Carly was beginning to understand the attraction that infatuation held for other women. Suddenly all her senses were sharpened; she could hear the steady rhythm of his breathing, she could still feel the warmth of his body against hers, picture the way his crystal-blue eyes could brighten like jewels when he looked at her. She inhaled, breathing in the scent of him—a rich, heady masculine scent that owed nothing to purchased cologne or expensive after-shave.

Oh, yes, she thought, resting her head against the cool pane of glass, there was something to be said for falling in love. Not that this was love, Carly assured herself. But it was so very, very beguiling.

Patrick had crossed the room to stand beside her. He watched her silently, viewing the emotions warring across the delicate planes of her face. She should be more circumspect, he considered with a detached sense of observation. Her lovely face was a mirror of her mind, allowing anyone to know precisely what she was thinking.

"Carly?"

She didn't answer, and for a moment Patrick wondered if she had heard him. Then she expelled a soft sigh, squared her shoulders with renewed determination and met his steady gaze.

"You're probably right," she admitted. "I think I would have made love with you today. Not that I'm in the habit of jumping into bed with every attractive man I meet," she rushed to add.

Although she knew it would allow him to realize how unreasonably he'd affected her, Carly didn't want Patrick to assume her behavior had been at all commonplace.

"I never thought that." He watched her hands tremble as they combed through the long hair skimming her shoulders. It was an intriguing mix of blond shades he knew to be natural, a deep honey laced with streaks of gold and another hue that reminded him of winter wheat under a gleaming sun.

"Good," she stated in a soft voice. She turned away again, idly drawing patterns in the condensation on the inside of the window. "I'll have to admit, Patrick, that was one of the most straightforward propositions I've ever received."

"I'm not a man who believes in coloring the issue with hearts and flowers," he stated flatly. "I want you, Carly. And unless every instinct I've got has gone on the blink, I'd say you feel the same way."

Carly didn't respond—there was no need. Her answer was as clear as if someone had taken a marking pen and written across her soft features in bold, black print.

Patrick's tone was gentler, but his eyes remained unreadable. "I can't tell you that we'll live happily ever after. But I do promise never to lie to you, Carly."

Everything was happening so fast. Carly shook her head, as if to clear it, and forced her expression to remain calm, her voice steady.

"Are you suggesting we have an affair?"

"I'm not suggesting anything," he contradicted in a conversational tone. "Since an affair between us is inevitable, I'm merely stating the ground rules."

Carly was far more shocked by the intensity of her own desire for Patrick than she was by his words, or his tone. Even now, when she should be demanding that he leave her apartment, she wanted him. The idea that anyone should have such power over another person was both intriguing and appalling.

"Since you're such a stickler for honesty," she stated, firming her resolve, as well as her spine, "let me give you an alternative set of rules."

"Go right ahead."

Carly's eyes flashed at his patronizing tone. "I have worked damn hard to create a life for myself, and at the moment, that life revolves around Capitol Airlines. The fact that you have some say in the outcome of that is, admittedly, a given. But you can't expect the same privilege outside the office. There'll be no affair, Patrick. I don't believe in mixing my personal life with my business."

"And if I don't like those rules?"

"Tough," she spat out, moving past him to retrieve his coat from the couch. "I think you've warmed up enough to go home now."

He took the overcoat she thrust at him, slipping it on as he cast a regretful look first at the warm fire, then at the blustery day outside the window. She was holding the door open, inviting him to leave, and with a careless shrug, he moved to comply.

Just when Carly thought she was home free, Patrick turned in the open doorway. "One more thing you should remember, sweetheart," he stated, his hands firmly on her shoulders, "is that I always make my own rules." Then he lowered his mouth to hers.

Carly had anticipated this kiss from the beginning. She had even fantasized about it during that erotic daydream in Lafayette Park. But never in her wildest imagination could she have suspected the effect it would have on her senses.

Never had she suspected that firm, unyielding mouth could be so gentle. A dizzying excitement raced through her as his lips moved over hers, tasting, teasing, persuading, but never demanding more than she was prepared to give. The kiss beguiled her, clouding her mind with a shimmering, golden glow that slowly infused itself throughout her body. When he circled her lips with the tip of his tongue, the light touch created a ring of exquisite lightning that remained even after he released her.

Something was wrong, Patrick realized, his heart pounding in his chest as he forced himself to back away from the tempting situation. He still wanted her. And from the way Carly had trembled in his arms, he knew he was not the only one affected by the sexual chemistry that had sparked between them from the beginning. He suspected that walking away would be difficult.

"I have to go," he said abruptly. Her delicate hands were still splayed against his chest and as he pulled them from his body, Patrick experienced an inexplicable sense of loss.

Carly's eyes were wide, still shadowed with unsatiated desire. Patrick watched, intrigued, as she struggled to concentrate on his words.

"Of course." She was proud of the calm tone she'd mustered from somewhere. "You must have a great deal to do. I imagine taking over an airline must entail mountains of paperwork."

Her anger he had been able to deal with. Her sarcasm had rolled off him like water off a duck's back; he'd been called far worse things than a corporate shark. But Patrick was stunned at how the veiled look of betrayal in her eyes pained him.

"You've got it all wrong, Carly. I'm spending this weekend moving."

"Back to New York?"

Carly wondered why she found that idea so distressing. She hadn't wanted him to come here in the first place and she certainly didn't want him to stay in Washington. Did she?

"Across town," he corrected. "I've leased a furnished house in Georgetown."

"Either you've money to burn, or you plan on staying for some time." She tried to keep the question from her voice, but failed.

"I assured you last night that I'm not the shark you think I am. My plans for Capitol are more complex than a simple takeover. You're not going to get rid of me that easily, lady."

As he looked inclined to kiss her once again, Carly wondered whether Patrick was referring to their business relationship or their personal one. She wasn't to be given a clue as he suddenly released her hands and walked out the door. It wasn't until he'd disappeared into the elevator that Carly realized she'd been holding her breath.

If there was one emotion that Carly never permitted herself, it was self-pity. She had learned at a very young age that no good ever came from sitting around feeling sorry for yourself. Her grandfather had always looked on the bright side of life, insisting that Carly do likewise.

When she had come home from school in the third grade, crying because the other students had teased her about not having a mother to bring to the Mother's Day play, the old man had allowed a few minutes of heartfelt tears. Then he'd pulled a bouquet of yellow daisies from his sleeve, coaxing an unwilling smile to her quivering lips. Finally, he had assured her that he'd known about the play and had arranged for Millie, his buxom assistant, to go in her mother's place. Even at the tender age of eight, Carly had been aware that the other mothers were shocked by Millie's dyed platinum hair and leopard-skin-printed dress. But she hadn't minded. Instead, she had found comfort in the fact that there were two people in the world who truly loved her.

"So what magic would you pull out of your hat for me this time, Gramps?" she murmured as she put an Oscar Peterson album on the stereo. Pouring a snifter of brandy, she settled down on the couch to stare into the flickering flames of the fire.

The blues of the jazz piano suited her mood perfectly as she wallowed in atypical self-pity. She knew she should be furious with Patrick Ryan. He was an arrogant, egotistical man who was probably going to ruin Bill's life and make her miserable doing so. But she couldn't forget how right his arms had felt around her, how his kiss had sparked a depth of emotion she had thought herself incapable of feeling.

"Damn him all to hell," she muttered, glaring at the rough-hewn masculine features she pictured in the red and orange flames. "From now on, I'm not going to give him a second thought. He can take Capitol, for all I care. But he isn't going to have me."

She continued to tell herself that as the room darkened with the purple shadows of dusk. Instead of turning on the lights, she continued to add logs to the fire, rising only to refill her glass or to put on another soulful record. Finally, discovering that banishing Patrick from her mind was an impossible task, she made her way into the bedroom. As she tossed and turned in a fitful sleep, Patrick Ryan's crystal-blue eyes continued to mock her throughout the night.

THE SHRILL DEMAND of the telephone shattered her sleep. Carly reached out blindly, fumbling for the receiver.

"H'llo?" she mumbled.

"I woke you," Patrick said apologetically.

"Of course you didn't," Carly lied, stifling a groan as she sat up in bed. Her head seemed to be filled with rocks, huge boulders that tumbled about with the slightest movement. She glanced over at her clock radio. "I'm always up at six on a Sunday morning. You never know who might phone. What are you calling for, anyway?"

"Would you believe I called to apologize about yesterday?"

"No," she answered promptly. "Not unless you had an ulterior motive for doing so."

Patrick bit back an oath. "You really don't trust me very much, do you?"

"No farther than I could throw you."

Patrick ignored her pointed accusation. "I need to talk to you before tomorrow morning."

"So talk."

Patrick reminded himself that Carly was not a woman to accept ultimatums. Persuasion was definitely in order. "I don't want to discuss it over the phone. Why don't you come over here? I'll fix breakfast," he offered expansively.

At the mere mention of food, Carly's stomach protested. "I'm not hungry."

He tried again. "I make a mean cup of coffee."

"Why are you being so nice to me all of a sudden?"

"We got off to a rough start. I'd like an opportunity to get things back on an even keel."

"That's not necessary."

Patrick's patience was wearing thin. "Carly, it's imperative that I talk to you before tomorrow morning. Now you can either come over here or I'll show up at your place in ten minutes and we can continue this discussion in bed. Take your pick."

That idea was definitely discomforting. "Your place," Carly answered instantly. Rummaging through the drawer of her bedside table, she found a pen and scribbled the address Patrick rattled off onto the cover of a paperback novel.

"How did you know I was in bed?"

"Easy. You have a very sexy voice when you're just waking up, woman."

His deep voice created a warmth that began at her toes, filling her with its golden glow all the way to the top of her head. Carly sank back against the pillow, responding to his seductive huskiness in spite of herself.

"Oh," she said softly.

"Oh," he mimicked, not unkindly. Then his tone firmed. "Now if you know what's good for you, you'll get out of bed before I decide to put pleasure before business and come over there to join you."

Carly believed him. Her feet immediately hit the floor. "I'm up," she announced.

"You've got a half hour to get over here." Before Carly could argue, Patrick hung up.

His abrupt response was like a splash of ice water and as the annoying dial tone rang in her ear, she glared at the receiver. Slamming it down onto the cradle, she stomped from the room and spent the next five minutes scrubbing her body viciously under the harsh spray of the shower, as if she could expunge its mutinous desire for such a difficult, untrustworthy man.

As she drove through the deserted Sunday morning streets, Carly vowed that she would not, under any conditions, allow Patrick Ryan to get under her skin again. His deep voice could give her all the provocative invitations it liked, those crystal eyes could stare at her until doomsday, hinting at untold sensual delights. And his body could send as many messages as it wished. She wasn't interested. Not in the slightest, she assured herself firmly, slipping her hand in her pocket to squeeze the lucky coin her grandfather had given her over twenty years ago.

It wasn't that she was actually superstitious, Carly reflected. The metallic talisman simply made her feel as if her grandfather was somewhere close by.

She found Patrick's house without difficulty and despite her vow not to like anything about the man, Carly fell instantly in love with his home. The bright blue siding of the Victorian house was enhanced by gray shutters and white gingerbread trim. A row of stately boxwood lined the brick sidewalk and though nothing bloomed in the window boxes at present, she could imagine bright red geraniums adding a welcome accent.

Patrick had obviously been watching for her as he opened the door before she had a chance to lift the ornate knocker.

"You look just like Little Red Riding Hood," he said by way of greeting as he took in the sight of her in the scarlet hooded coat.

"I think I'll avoid the obvious comeback."

"Does that mean you've changed your mind about me?" His smile, if appealing, appeared false.

"No. It means that it was too easy," Carly stated blithely. "I prefer more of a challenge."

"If it's a challenge you're after, Carly, you've come to the right place. You'll have to make your way around the boxes, I'm afraid. I haven't had time to unpack anything but a few essentials."

"That's all right. Believe me, neatness is not my strong suit."

"That's a relief. I was afraid you'd be running your finger over the stairwells, looking for dust."

"Why on earth would I do that?"

Patrick shrugged. "Don't all women? In an attempt to prove how badly we poor mortal men need them in our lives?"

Carly laughed good-naturedly. "I hope I have more to offer a man than my cleaning talents. Because if it all comes down to how shiny my kitchen floor is, I'm destined to a life of spinsterhood."

Patrick had been making his way to the kitchen at the back of the house. At Carly's words he turned, his hands deep in the front pockets of his jeans as he eyed her thoughtfully.

"I don't think you have to concern yourself with being an old maid, Carly. Any man who allows himself to fall in love with you isn't going to be worrying about your housekeeping skills."

Carly was shaken by the almost angry seriousness of his tone. What a funny way to put it, she mused, trying to read some message in his hooded eyes. He'd said "allow" himself to fall in love. As if a person could control such things. She sighed inwardly. If what Patrick was doing to her was any indication, mere mortals had no power whatsoever over such an ethereal thing as falling in love.

"Is that a compliment?" she asked softly.

For just one fleeting moment his expression gentled, his eyes warmed. "I suppose it is," he admitted, feeling unreasonably like a boy just hitting puberty.

Every atom in his body was all too aware of Carly's femininity. She had unbuttoned her coat as she'd entered the house and his gaze riveted on the way her breasts rose and fell under the kelly-green sweater. The soft wool of her navy slacks hugged her curves, outlining long, firm legs that he longed to feel wrapped around his body.

She was driving him crazy; she'd caused him to go two nights without sleep, and he was finding it impossible to concentrate with that enticing cloud of white roses and jasmine that surrounded her. Telling himself that it was the only way they were going to get any work done, Patrick vowed to have her before the day was out.

"Thank you, Patrick." She managed a friendly smile. "I think I'll accept that compliment, since it's probably the only one I'll ever get from you."

Carly was not unaware of Patrick's desire; nor could she deny her own answering response. His gaze had created a fluttering deep within her, like a butterfly spreading its wings, and she wanted nothing more than to allow what she knew would be an unequaled experience. But even as she admitted her own sexual hunger, Carly realized that something else was happening between her and Patrick. Something she couldn't yet put a name to.

Certain that it was more than mere lust, she couldn't accept the idea that she and Patrick Ryan could possibly be falling in love on such brief acquaintance. Besides, he wasn't her type. She preferred the men in her life to be more easygoing, more manageable. Yet something was definitely occurring between them that had little or nothing to do with their enforced business alliance.

She thrust her hand into her pocket, absently stroking her lucky coin for courage, unaware of how the gesture pulled the wool even tighter against her hips.

"Don't count on that," Patrick said eventually. His voice was unnaturally hoarse. "You're a woman who inspires compliments."

Enough was enough, Carly decided. She enjoyed flirting as much as any woman, but flirting with Patrick Ryan was like playing with a hand grenade after the pin had been pulled.

"Do you have any aspirin?" she asked abruptly. "I ran out last week and never got to the drugstore. And could I get that cup of coffee you promised? I can't think straight in the morning until my third cup."

Patrick was both grateful for the sudden change in subject and irritated by the way she'd deftly slipped out of the net of desire that had settled over them. Oh, well, he considered, they had a long day of work ahead of them. He could set about seducing the lovely Carly Ashton this evening, over a romantic dinner and a bottle of good wine.

Not that it would really be a seduction. Whether she wanted to admit it or not, Patrick knew Carly recognized the inevitability of their affair. They were like two freight trains speeding toward each other on the same track and nothing was going to stop the impending collision.

"You look as if you're going to need more than a few cups of coffee," Patrick observed casually, eyeing her red-rimmed eyes.

"I think I'm coming down with a cold," Carly lied.

Patrick wasn't fooled for a moment. He could recognize the lingering effects of a hangover, having suffered a few of his own over the years. Satisfied that he hadn't been the only one to spend a long, miserable night, he decided not to press the issue. She was probably suffering enough.

"It's that time of the year," he said noncommittally as he turned on his heel and continued toward the kitchen.

Carly followed. She tossed her coat onto an extra chair as she settled down at the table, gratefully taking the steaming cup of coffee he handed her.

"Thank you."

"You're welcome."

After refilling his own cup, Patrick opened the refrigerator he had stocked yesterday and took out a carafe of tomato juice. Rummaging through the paper bags still lining the counter, he pulled out several items that he mixed into a tall glass.

"Here." He put the drink down in front of her along with two white tablets.

Carly observed the unappetizing mixture suspiciously. The color of rust, it smelled even less appealing than it looked.

"What's this? Hemlock?"

"A guaranteed cure for colds."

"I think I'll stick to chicken soup, thank you." She continued to sip the hot coffee, willing her body to come alive.

Patrick didn't bother to hide his frustration. He'd never met such an intransigent woman. "Look, Carly, we've got a long day ahead of us and you look like hell. Your eyes remind me of a map of the LA freeway system, and you don't have any color in your cheeks." He picked up the glass, holding it toward her. "Drink up. I need you in tip-top shape."

"You've got a real way with words," she muttered, reluctantly accepting the murky concoction.

Knowing he'd spoken too harshly, Patrick softened his tone. "I stand corrected. If you were in any better shape, I'd never be able to concentrate on work. It's going to be difficult enough as it is."

Refusing to acknowledge the light gleaming in his eyes, Carly popped the aspirin into her mouth and took a long swallow of the juice, choking on the bitter taste.

"What's in this stuff, anyway?" she gasped, wiping her mouth with the back of her hand.

"It's a secret recipe."

"Now I know what formaldehyde tastes like," she muttered.

"You can always try holding your nose," Patrick suggested amiably. "That's what I always do. When I've got a cold," he tacked on wickedly, letting her know that he was well aware of her condition. "Finish it, Carly. I guarantee you'll feel like a new woman."

"Or a dead one," she countered grimly. Nevertheless, she threw her head back and swallowed the rest of the thick, caustic brew. "God," she groaned, "if this is any example of your culinary talents, I'm glad I passed on breakfast."

Her gaze dropped to the papers scattered over the table. There were several ledger sheets, notes scribbled in a bold, black script in the margins. The nearly empty coffeepot, plus the shadows under Patrick's eyes suggested that he had been at work most of the night.

"You're serious about Capitol, aren't you?" she asked with a sinking feeling.

Patrick didn't answer her question directly, but his expression told Carly more than his words. "I'm not going to lie to you. Bill told me that you've been doing a lot of his work lately; that being the case, you know Capitol's situation as well as anyone. You're losing money every day; the situation is ripe for a takeover."

"We weren't the only airline to lose money last year," she argued.

"True. Just as you won't be the only one to file for bankruptcy."

Carly's cup had been on the way to her lips, but at his words, her numb fingers released their hold and hot coffee spilled onto her lap.

4

DAMN," CARLY CRIED OUT, jumping up from the table. "Now look what you've made me do!"

Knowing that her distress was due more to the idea of bankruptcy than spilled coffee, Patrick refrained from answering. He pulled a roll of paper towels from a paper bag. Tearing off a long piece, he began to dab her slacks.

"I'm perfectly capable of doing that myself, Mr. Ryan."

Carly yanked the towels from his hands and scrubbed viciously at the dark stain.

Patrick sat down, calmly waiting for Carly's temper to subside. The air was rife with antagonism, and sparks were practically arcing about her blond head. Patrick was surprised to find himself affected by her obvious distress and wondered what it was about Carly Ashton that made him wish they had met under other circumstances.

Finally, all fight seemed to drain out of her and Carly sank back onto the ladderback chair, her fingers tracing nervous, unhappy designs on the tabletop.

"I don't want to file," she said softly.

"You don't have any choice."

As Carly's features settled into hard, argumentative lines, Patrick reminded himself that to bulldoze over her feelings would not solve anything. That she had no choice was obvious, but too much depended on her cooperation. He'd have to make her see things his way. He reached across the table, covering her hand with his.

"Look, Carly, all we're doing is utilizing Chapter 11 to protect Capitol from the creditors while we reorganize. It's not like we're using some federal loophole to stiff anyone."

She frowned. "I still don't like the idea."

"It's the only way. Especially now. I have every reason to believe that the machinists are going out on strike. If that happens, your creditors will swoop down on you like a pack of hungry vultures."

Carly jerked her hand free and glared across the table at him. "How do you know the machinists are going to strike? They're not voting until late this afternoon."

"Believe me, Carly, the vote will be to strike."

"I didn't realize you had a crystal ball."

Patrick bit back his instinctive retort as he waved away her sarcasm. He couldn't remember the last time he had lost his temper. But Carly's dogged resistance had him closer to exploding than he had been in years.

"It doesn't matter how I know. What matters is that we are prepared to protect Capitol against the fallout when it happens."

Carly studied him thoughtfully, hating the fact that his words made sense. "I suppose you're right."

Patrick experienced no satisfaction at her surrender. This was the easy part. He had a feeling how she was going to react when she heard the rest of his news.

"You know, I really hate this," Carly continued. "When I first went to work with Bill, he promised that I'd be responsible for press releases, customer relations and convincing travel agents that we're a wonderful airline. That's what I love—the people part of the business. That's what I'm good at."

A small, rippling sigh escaped her lips. "Instead I've been poring over balance sheets, analyzing routes, arguing with disgruntled union representatives who refuse to admit that there might possibly be two sides to every issue. But even when I manage to solve a problem, two more pop up to take its place."

Patrick remained silent, watching as she unconsciously twisted the gold ring on her finger. Better to let her talk, he decided. To let her get it all out. He had the impression that it had been a very long time since Carly had felt free to discuss her troubles with anyone. Once again Patrick found himself wondering at the relationship between Carly Ashton and her absent partner.

Her voice was soft, barely above a whisper in the quiet room. "I feel as if I've got my finger in the dike and if I allow myself to relax, even for a moment, we'll all be washed away in the resulting flood."

A crooked, self-deprecating smile curved her lips. "Whatever happened to the days when my biggest problem was what magazines we'd carry on board? Or deciding what promotional items to give away to travel agents at their annual conventions?"

Her words drifted off as Carly realized she was confirming Patrick's opinion that Bill had not been fulfilling his duties.

"Speaking of travel agents," she said as a thought occurred to her, "if we file for Chapter 11, it's bound to hurt our bookings. How are we going to continue to fly without passengers?"

"You're already losing bookings because travel agents are nervous about the possibility of discontinued flights," Patrick reminded her. "And don't forget, the insurance protecting those agents against losses on Capitol's tickets in the event you cease operating expires in six weeks. Without protection, I can't see it being renewed. Can you?"

"You've certainly done your homework, haven't you?"

"It's my business," he pointed out. "But if I didn't feel there was a chance to pull this off, I wouldn't be here."

Not for the first time, Carly considered that were she to search the world seeking a white knight to rescue Capitol Airlines, Patrick Ryan would undoubtedly be her last choice. But as hard as she tried, Carly couldn't come up with a workable alternative.

"What do you suggest?" she asked, her shoulders slumped with resignation.

"First, cancel all overseas flights. The strong dollar is killing you in the foreign marketplace. Too much of your revenue is in foreign currencies."

"That makes sense." Carly had never agreed with Bill's expansion into the overseas market, anyway.

"Next, sell off some of the planes to acquire some fast, much needed cash. You can't borrow any deeper into your credit line."

Carly's lips firmed. "The unions will love that. Do you realize how many people we'd have to lay off?"

He waved away her protest. "They'll buy it because they won't have any choice."

Privately, Carly thought Patrick was being overly optimistic, but instead of arguing the point, she brought up another objection.

"Selling off planes will reduce capacity," she argued. "If we're short on capacity, not only will we lose passengers, but we won't be able to maintain decent schedules, so we'll lose even more passengers. Exactly how is that supposed to help?"

"Order some new Airbus Industrie jets."

Carly held her ground. "It'll take years to get delivery."

Patrick was undeterred by the glittering challenge in her blue eyes. "So you lease some for the interim period. What Capitol needs to do is reduce the type of aircraft it flies. At present you're flying six different types. Cutting that down to two or three will reduce training, maintenance and spare-parts costs. The new fleet will burn less fuel, and the Airbus jets only require two-man crews instead of the three you're using now."

It made sense, Carly admitted silently. Except for one thing. "Every suggestion you've made so far reduces the number of employees. What on earth makes you think the unions will go along with that?"

She was on her feet, pacing the floor, twisting her hands together as she considered the mess they were in. Carly desperately wished Bill was here. Oh, not as he'd been the past two years, but strong and decisive. The way he'd been when she had entered into this partnership.

He'd had such big plans, she thought sadly, remembering how he had stunned the aviation world when it looked as if he was actually going to pull those plans off. Despite the warnings about Sir Freddy Laker's inability to keep an airline flying by himself, Bill had been well on the way to proving all the doubting Thomases wrong. Until Meredith's accident.

She pressed her palms down against the butcher block counter, staring unseeingly out the window, oblivious to the softly falling snow drifting down like a scene from a Currier and Ives print. Her long blond hair fell forward, and though Patrick couldn't see her face, he could read defeat in her stance. It was now or never, he decided, taking a deep breath.

"The unions will go along with the deal because they're going to have a stake in the outcome," he said.

She shook her head. "We're in no position to offer incentives. You know as well as I do that there isn't a penny available for increased salaries or benefits."

"That's not what I had in mind. You're going to let the employees buy into Capitol, Carly. That's the only way."

She turned abruptly. "That's what this is all about, isn't it? That's how you know about the strike vote. You're working for the unions. With them." She didn't bother to conceal her scorn.

"Not exactly." He rose from his chair and moved toward her.

Carly tried to back away, but found her progress stopped by the counter. He placed his hands on the butcher block, framing her body, forestalling escape.

I could kick him, Carly considered wildly, casting a quick glance down at those long legs that were too close to hers for comfort.

"I wouldn't try it," he warned.

"Try what?"

"You know what. And believe me, I'd just crawl after you and tackle you before you made it to the front door."

"You can't read my mind," she snapped. "I happen to know for a fact that mind reading is nothing but a hoax."

"I'm not reading your mind."

She arched an argumentative brow. "Oh?"

"Actually, I was reading your eyes. Did you know they turn purple when you get angry?"

"They're blue," she argued. "Dark blue."

He leaned his head a little closer. "They look purple to me. Like pansies."

As his breath wafted across her lips, Carly drank in a minty taste she guessed to be toothpaste, along with the scent of rich, dark coffee. Although he hadn't touched her, she could feel the warmth of his body penetrating her thick sweater and slacks, and once again she experienced those unruly desires deep within her all too responsive body.

"This is a ridiculous conversation," she muttered.

One minute they had been discussing Capitol Airlines like two professionals, and the next minute all pretense had dropped away and they were once more engaged in that age-old battle of the sexes. Carly reminded herself to think of Capitol, to consider how this traitor was planning to ruin her life, as well as Bill's. She couldn't let him get away with it without a fight.

"Besides," she spat out, returning the conversation to their initial topic, "if you have your way, you'll go home with the grand prize, won't you? Your very own airline to go along with all those electronic companies and manufacturing plants."

Patrick ignored her accusation as he reached out to tuck a thick swath of hair behind her ear. Carly found herself trapped by his treacherously tender gaze. And his touch. Oh, dear Lord, she considered weakly, as his fingers splayed against her throat, what power did this man possess that he could create such longing within her?

Patrick read the answering desire in her eyes, just as he could read the lingering dread. He could have her. But when Carly Ashton gave herself to him, he wanted it to be without reservations. Even if her body was definitely willing to take whatever he had to offer, her mind was still rejecting intimacy. Despite the fact that she was driving him crazy, Patrick found himself vowing to breach that final barrier, no matter how long it took.

He slowly backed away, shaking his head. "You're too beautiful for your own good," he said regretfully. "You make a man think of things he has no business considering."

Carly was still suffering from the anticipation of a kiss that had never come and she met his grim expression with wide, passion-laced eyes.

"I don't know what you're talking about," she protested. "One minute we were arguing over your plans for Capitol and the next..." Her voice drifted off as she realized she was about to reveal far more than she wanted Patrick to know.

"The next we were imagining making love," he filled in for her. His eyes were distractingly devoid of emotion.

"You take too much for granted," she said briskly, walking toward the kitchen door. She scooped her coat up as she passed the apple-green ladderback chair.

"Do I?"

Carly shrugged on the coat, flipping up the hood as she turned in the doorway to look back at him. "Yes, you do," she insisted. "About me. And about Capitol. I'm calling Bill as soon as I get home," she warned heatedly. "Believe me, Mr. Ryan, we're going to fight you tooth and nail on this one."

Once again, Patrick experienced that odd flash of jealousy at the way her tone had softened on her partner's name. He knew it was dirty pool, but reminded himself that no victory had ever gone to the meek.

"I wouldn't count on it," he drawled uncaringly. "Because McIntyre knows what I plan to do. And he's behind me. Every step of the way."

His words struck like a fist into her midsection, and Carly leaned weakly against the doorframe. "I don't believe it."

Patrick felt like the bastard he knew she thought him to be as he watched the color leave her creamy complexion. *That was a low blow, Ryan,* he told himself. But in this case, the ends justified the means. Still, he hated watching the comprehension slowly dawn in those beautiful violet eyes, finally to be replaced with a deep expression of betrayal. Patrick wondered who'd dealt her the harsher blow. McIntyre or himself? Neither choice gave him any comfort.

"That's what I wanted to talk to you about," he said finally. "I've already received board approval to do whatever is necessary to save Capitol. In the meantime, McIntyre has agreed to take a leave of absence."

"I don't believe that! Bill started Capitol; he had such hopes for its success; he'd never turn it over to you willingly."

"The announcement will be made tomorrow morning," Patrick stated quietly. "I felt it only fair to let you know ahead of time."

"Fair?" Carly asked incredulously. "You're a fine one to talk about fairness, Patrick Ryan. Do you realize what this will do to Bill?"

Patrick forced an uncaring shrug. "He'll survive. The man has been around long enough to know he'd run out of options."

Carly gave him a fierce look. "You are a bastard," she accused heatedly. "For your information, Bill's life has been a living hell ever since—"

She spun on her heel, heading for the front door. "Forget it," she ground out. "You're the last person capable of understanding emotional pain or human failing!"

For a moment Patrick couldn't move. His feet seemed to be bolted to the floor as cold waves of despair washed over him. Oh, he knew pain all right. He'd been on intimate terms with it. Patrick didn't know whether it was the memory of Julia's death or the idea that Carly honestly believed he was incapable of human feelings that made him feel so miserable. The sound of the front door slamming shattered his introspection and he headed after her on a run.

She had parked her red Mustang two doors down the cobblestone street. Patrick caught up with her before she reached the car.

"Carly, wait a minute!"

She shook his hand off her arm as she glared up at him.

"You're not going to take it away, do you hear me? I'll fight you every step of the way, Patrick. I'll get proxies, I'll run ads in the *Wall Street Journal*, I'll go on television talk shows. I'll tell Jane Pauley and David Hartman and Phil Donahue what a rat you are.... And Ted Koppel. So help me God, I'll get on *Nightline* and I'll tell the world what a low-down—"

In desperation, Patrick did the only thing he could think of to still her diatribe. He cut her off with a furious kiss. The wind had picked up, swirling the falling snow around them, but they were lost in a storm of their own making as tempers flared into a kiss of unbridled passion. Her hood fell back and Patrick thrust his hands into her hair, holding her to his hungry mouth, demanding submission. Carly's own lips were greedy, as if she were determined to exact a punishment of her own for Patrick's betrayal.

How could she want him, she asked herself. How could she need him so desperately, knowing what he was? What he intended to do?

It was black magic, she decided, gasping as his tongue thrust deep into her mouth, twining itself around hers. Her grandfather's magic had consisted of sleight of hand, tricks, illusions. But this was the real thing. Dark, dangerous and so powerful that she thought she might die from the savage forces surging through her.

Patrick had never meant things to get out of hand so quickly. At first, he'd only intended to quiet her so he could coax her back into the house in order to explain. When she'd ceased fighting him and begun to cooperate fully in the kiss, he'd allowed himself the pleasure of her uninhibited response.

But his heart had begun to pound unsteadily, his head was spinning from the unbridled hunger of Carly's demanding kiss, and he felt himself standing near the edge of a dark, forbidding pit.

"Another minute and we're going to get arrested," he said huskily. His breath was uneven as he fought for control.

Carly stared at him. The scattered snowflakes gracing his dark hair and thick lashes belatedly reminded her where they were. And who they were. Combatants in a battle she had vowed not to let him win.

It suddenly occurred to Carly that there might be a way out of all this. What was to prevent her from hearing Patrick's plans for Capitol, then carrying them out herself? It was worth a try.

"You're going to catch your death of cold," she said.

"You were doing a pretty good job of keeping me warm."

"Go back into the house, Patrick," Carly instructed with far more aplomb than she was feeling at the moment. "You're not even wearing a coat." She turned to leave, but he caught her arm, spinning her back against him.

"We need to talk."

"We can talk at the office. Tomorrow," she insisted.

"I thought you cared about what happened to Capitol."

"You already have the bankruptcy papers drawn up to file with the court, don't you?"

"Of course."

Carly nodded. She wasn't at all surprised. It appeared the board had given Patrick carte blanche. She would have to change that. But not now. Not until she could convince the board members that they didn't need Patrick Ryan. She'd have to talk to Bill. It was imperative that he realize the need to put up a fight.

"Well," Carly stated in a brisk, businesslike tone, "since we can't file until tomorrow morning, I'd say you have everything well under control."

She turned away, and this time Patrick made no move to stop her. Instead he jammed his hands into his pockets. "Are you always this stubborn?"

Carly flashed him a quick smile, as false as the ones he'd given her. "Not at all," she answered blithely. "Most people find me quite charming and easygoing. You must bring out the worst in me."

She unlocked her car door, got into the compact Mustang and pulled away from the curb. When she dared to glance in her rearview mirror, she saw Patrick still standing on the sidewalk, a thoughtful expression on his face.

CARLY FINALLY TRACKED BILL DOWN at the clinic in Vermont where Meredith was undergoing rehabilitation therapy. A devastating car accident had left the young woman unable to walk, and Bill had spent the past two years taking his daughter to one specialist after another. His obsession with Meredith had eclipsed his astute business sense and Carly had been forced to stand by helplessly as Bill spent less and less time in Capitol's Washington headquarters.

"Carly," he greeted her cautiously, "this is a surprise."

"Not nearly as large as the one I've just received," she countered. Then, remembering where he was, Carly forced her mind away from her immediate problem.

"How's Meredith?" she questioned, preparing herself for the worst.

"I think we're finally on the right track," Bill answered slowly.

Carly knew he didn't want to allow himself any false hope. There had been too many disappointments during the past two years.

"The surgery last month seems to have been successful," he continued. "When Elaine and I arrived, she was with her physiotherapist. They've detected some motor movement in her left leg."

Despite her distress, Carly smiled. "I'm glad to hear that. She deserves some good luck. You all do."

"You can say that again." There was a little pool of silence. "But you didn't call to talk about Meredith, did you, Carly?"

She felt a little guilty even bringing the subject up. Taking a deep breath, Carly attempted to choose her words carefully. "I had an interesting conversation with Patrick Ryan earlier. Is it true you're taking a leave of absence?"

She could hear her friend's heavy sigh over the long-distance wires. "I'm afraid so, sugar."

"You can't just give up like this," Carly argued. "Not after all the time and effort you've put into Capitol. You can't just walk away and turn it over to that...that Wall Street shark!"

"I didn't have any choice, Carly," Bill countered. "The man is our only hope for saving the airline. The board is behind him one hundred percent. They also agree that at this point in time, my presence would complicate matters. In order for the unions to negotiate with Ryan, they have to understand that he's the man in charge."

Inwardly, Carly admitted the strategy made sense. Still, she found the circumstances distinctly unpalatable. "Was the board vote unanimous?"

"There were a few dissenters in the beginning," he admitted reluctantly.

"I'm not at all surprised," she muttered. "What did he do, hold a gun to their heads? Threaten to hold their children hostage until they agreed to his demands?"

"Nothing that dramatic. If you want to know the truth, I convinced them Ryan was our only protection against a hostile takeover."

"*You* convinced them? Why?"

"I don't want Capitol to end up in the hands of our competitors," he explained patiently. "Ryan can keep that from happening."

"He can also take everything away from you," Carly pointed out. "What's to prevent him from freezing you out of your own company?"

"I trust him to be fair."

"Fair?" Carly's voice cracked. "What makes you think that word is even in the man's vocabulary?"

"He's already offered me a good price for my stock if I agree to take early retirement," Bill stated. "And promised me a seat on the board."

"As chairman?"

Bill coughed uncomfortably. "That item was left up in the air," he admitted. "That's why I made such a fool of myself Friday night, asking you to convince him to keep me on." His voice thickened. "Then I got up here and saw Meredith, and suddenly the entire matter didn't seem very important any longer. Right now I'm more concerned with my daughter's progress than I am with maintaining my seat of power."

Carly could understand that. She didn't like the implications of Bill's reasoning, but she could certainly understand that his family would come before his business. In that respect, Bill McIntyre had always stood head and shoulders above most of the other businessmen Carly was acquainted with. Most would not hesitate to sacrifice anyone or anything in order to achieve success. That was why she would always love Bill. That was also why she'd fight to her last breath to ensure that Capitol would be waiting for him to pick up the reins again, once this was all over.

"You're a good man, Bill McIntyre," she said softly.

He chuckled. "You're not real happy with me right now, are you, sugar?"

"It just all came as a bit of a shock," Carly hedged. "Why didn't you warn me?"

His voice displayed honest regret. "To tell you the truth, I couldn't bear to see the expression on your face. I'm afraid I took the coward's way out by letting Ryan break the news to you. . . . What do you really think of him?" Bill asked as an afterthought.

"He's arrogant, egotistical and insufferable," she answered immediately.

Again that deep chuckle. "I got the feeling he likes you, too. Who knows, Carly, maybe we'll get a merger offer out of this mess yet."

Carly smiled in spite of herself. "You're incorrigible. When are you going to stop trying to marry me off?"

"The day I have the honor of walking you down the aisle," Bill answered without missing a beat. "Carly, I've got to go. Elaine and I have a consultation with the doctor in a couple of minutes."

"Give Elaine my love. And tell Meredith I'm pulling for her."

Bill's voice turned husky with emotion. "I sure will. Take care of yourself, sugar. And don't worry about me. I've got more lives than an old barn cat."

As she hung up the telephone, Carly wished she could be as optimistic as Bill seemed to be about Patrick Ryan's presence.

Needing something to take her mind off her problems, Carly spent the remainder of the afternoon cleaning, working out her frustrations by scrubbing, vacuuming and polishing until her apartment was unnaturally tidy and smelled like a northern pine forest. Open heart surgery could have been done on her kitchen table, and even Mr. Clean would have envied the sheen on her bathroom tile.

That evening, after popping a frozen dinner into the microwave, she settled down on the sofa to watch a trashy, but admittedly engrossing, miniseries on television. Patrick Ryan belonged in Hollywood, she mused, forgetting her vow not to think of him until tomorrow morning. She knew that any of those women she was viewing on her nineteen-inch screen would jump at the chance to go to bed with him.

Actually, considering the travel his work entailed, Carly decided Patrick probably had an entire string of women from Seattle to Tallahassee and all points in between. Denver, Des

Moines, Detroit. He'd probably left no state untouched. So why did he want her? Although her vanity would have liked to attribute his motives to the fact that he found her irresistible, Carly was too pragmatic for that idea. She finally came to the conclusion that Patrick was simply one of those men who relished the thrill of the chase, achieving satisfaction with each additional woman's surrender.

"Well, not this time," she muttered, pointing her remote control at the screen, unable to take any more of the steamy love scenes. Her imagination had been working overtime as it was; it didn't need further stimulation.

Carly went to bed, vowing that no matter how appealing Patrick Ryan was, she was not about to become another notch on his headboard.

5

PATRICK'S PREDICTION regarding the machinists proved correct the next morning. Carly received the news along with the rest of the world on her car radio as she drove to the office.

Marge Kenyon, the secretary Carly shared with Bill, was waiting for her in the office. The vivid slash of burgundy blusher could not hide Marge's unnaturally pale coloring.

"Is it true? Are we declaring bankruptcy?" she asked Carly anxiously.

Carly hung up her coat. "Bad news certainly has a way of traveling fast," she murmured.

"But is it true?" Marge repeated.

"I'm afraid so," Carly admitted as she perched on a corner of her desk. She held up a hand as Marge opened her mouth to protest. "But it's not as bad as it sounds. We're only protecting Capitol while we reorganize. Things should continue as normal around here. Hopefully, a lot better," she amended.

Marge tilted her head in the direction of Bill's office, next door to Carly's. "Are you calling him normal?"

"Him?" Carly had an uneasy feeling exactly who they were talking about. The idea that Patrick Ryan had already set up camp in Bill's office created a flare of renewed irritation. "I suppose you're talking about Mr. Ryan."

"He was here when I arrived," Marge confirmed. "He seems very nice.... You should see his eyes."

"I've seen them," Carly answered dryly. "Personally, I found them remarkably ordinary. Just like everything else about the man."

Marge stared. "I think you need your own eyes examined, Carly. The man is gorgeous."

"To each his own," Carly responded uncaringly. "I just hope you find him as charming when you have to work with him. He seems a bit too overbearing for my taste."

"He made his own coffee," Marge offered as proof of Patrick's agreeability. Then she frowned as Carly's words sank in. "Then it's also true about Mr. McIntyre being fired? I couldn't believe that one."

"Good. Because it's not true. Bill has simply taken a leave of absence to be with his daughter. Mr. Ryan has graciously agreed to step into the breach."

"How is Meredith?"

"When I talked with Bill yesterday, he sounded encouraged."

"I'm glad. Mr. McIntyre needs a strong dose of good luck these days." Marge's words echoed Carly's own thoughts. "Then I'm not going to lose my job?"

"Of course not," Carly answered instantly. "You know we couldn't run this place without you, Marge."

The secretary returned Carly's smile. "I'm glad to hear that. You won't believe the rumors making the rounds this morning."

"We'll have to do something to clear them up," Carly murmured thoughtfully. "Perhaps we should have a meeting to give Mr. Ryan an opportunity to explain everything."

"That's a good idea," Marge agreed. "Just let me know what time and I'll see everyone gets the word."

"I'll do that," Carly answered as she slid off the desk and headed toward the door.

Not for the first time, Carly thanked her lucky stars for Marge Kenyon as she went down the hall. Despite a figure that had the men employees constantly walking into walls and a face that belonged on the cover of a fashion magazine, the woman was intelligent, discreet and possessed a talent for organization that Carly had often envied. She was really more an administrative assistant than a secretary and Carly had recently asked Bill to grant her both a raise and a promotion. While Bill had seen merit in Carly's suggestion, he had professed that he didn't want to lose Marge to middle management. Despite her continued arguments concerning the unfairness of that position, Bill hadn't budged.

"Couldn't you even wait for the body to get cold?" Carly snapped as she entered the executive office to find Patrick already in residence, his papers spread all over Bill McIntyre's wide desk.

He arched a dark brow above the frame of the reading glasses perched on his straight nose. "I didn't think we had time for formalities," he shot back. "As it is, I spent half the night with Clayton, getting his assurance the machinists will give us two weeks before walking out."

She couldn't help noticing he had said "us," uniting them in their battle to save Capitol. Could it be that he wasn't as ruthless as she had first thought? That idea, combined with the fact that the shadows she viewed under his eyes behind the lenses were even darker than yesterday, made Carly regret her waspish tone. The man must have been working around the clock since arriving in Washington.

"I should have been there with you."

Patrick smiled, all earlier traces of irritation disappearing. "You should have been with me," he agreed. "But for those lonely hours I didn't spend arguing with an ill-tempered union rep."

Leaning back in the leather chair, he pulled off the glasses, taking a slow, complete study of her. "Do you always wear such vivid colors?"

"I've never given it much thought. But now that you mention it, I suppose I do prefer bright shades. Why?" she asked, suddenly suspicious. This was not a man who made idle conversation.

"I was just wondering. I like it. That cheery yellow sweater is like having my very own private sun to warm a dreary day."

Carly held up a hand in a warning gesture. "Watch it," she advised. "You're treading on dangerous ground."

"Because I said I liked your sweater?" Patrick asked incredulously. "Come on, Carly, that's an innocent enough observation."

At his self-righteous expression, Carly backed down. "I suppose it is. So long as you weren't getting personal."

"I wasn't in the slightest," he answered instantly. Just when she had decided to believe him, devils began dancing in his clear blue eyes. "Now if I'd mentioned how delightful I find that enticing body *under* the sunshine-yellow sweater, you might have some grounds for complaint."

"Patrick!"

"I was only speaking hypothetically, Carly," he responded guilelessly.

"God help us all," she muttered as she poured herself a cup of coffee from the warmer on a nearby counter.

Carly was rapidly discovering precisely how Patrick maneuvered all those business dealings to his advantage. The man was as slippery as an eel. And every bit as dangerous.

"Do you believe in reincarnation?" she asked suddenly, pinning him with a particularly sagacious gaze.

"I don't think so. Why?"

"I was just considering the possibility that in a former life you were a riverboat gambler," she allowed. "I can see you with a rakish black mustache, dressed in a ruffled white shirt and string tie, shuffling the cards while banjos are strumming 'Dixie' in the background."

He stretched his long legs out in front of him, a satisfied smile on his face. "I think I like that image," Patrick decided. "Am I winning?"

"Oh, you always win," Carly agreed.

"I've always been lucky."

"Of course. It also helps that you cheat whenever necessary."

Refraining from responding to her challenge, Patrick eyed her thoughtfully. "And what were you in your past life, Carly?" he asked, falling into her game. He rubbed his chin. "A courtesan, perhaps? A Gypsy?" His eyes sparkled as he seemed to be giving the matter a great deal of consideration. "Were you perchance a witch?"

"Now that is complimentary," she complained.

"I meant it to be. I can easily imagine you casting spells over any man foolish enough to get within incantation range."

There it was again. That less than subtle statement that Patrick was a man who avoided personal entanglements at all costs. Reminding herself that was precisely what she wanted, Carly tried not to be offended.

"You're still way off base," she stated, sitting down in a chair on the visitor's side of the wide desk. "I would have been a dance hall girl," she was shocked to find herself admitting. "Dancing the cancan in some boomtown saloon." What was it about Patrick Ryan that encouraged her to reveal such private thoughts?

Patrick rejected that idea immediately. "Uh-uh."

"Why not? I'll have you know I'm a very good dancer. And I love adventure." And love, she reminded herself, was undeniably the ultimate adventure.

"I'm not denying your skill or your charm. I just think that if I'm to be included in this fantasy, I'd prefer you dancing on my riverboat."

His friendly smile momentarily disarmed Carly. "The *Delta Queen*," she agreed. "A paddle steamer on the Mississippi."

"That's better. At least in the middle of the river you'd have no place to run when a certain rakish gambler staked his claim."

Patrick's husky tone threatened to be her undoing once again, and Carly wondered what on earth had possessed her to begin this silly game in the first place. She and her grandfather had often indulged in fanciful daydreams. But she should have known better to allow such errant thoughts in the presence of Patrick Ryan.

"It's a big boat." She dismissed the subject by avoiding his eyes as she lifted her cup to her lips.

Patrick had never considered himself a fanciful or wishful person. But then again, he admitted, Carly had a way of bringing out a great many feelings he was not used to experiencing. Taking her pointed cue, he reluctantly turned the conversation back to their immediate problem.

"Tell me about McIntyre," he instructed with more force than he'd planned.

Carly slowly lowered her cup and gave him a long, level gaze. "It's not my place. Anything you want to know about Bill, you can ask him yourself."

"That's difficult to do when the man is snowbound in Vermont," Patrick pointed out grittily.

"Snowbound?"

"They're having a blizzard up there. I tried to call him this morning, just to let him know what was happening, but all the lines were down."

Carly was certain she had misunderstood him. "You were going to keep Bill abreast of things?" she asked softly. "Even though you manipulated his departure?"

He shrugged. "That was a necessary move. As for letting him know about the negotiations, I'm not unreasonable, Carly. I can appreciate that the guy might want to know what's happening with his airline."

Before Carly could open her mouth to admit she found that surprisingly thoughtful, Patrick's expression hardened. "Now start talking, Carly. Because unless you manage to change my mind in the next few hours, your partner's going to find himself on his way out of Capitol Airlines. Without any golden parachute to assist in a soft landing."

Carly drew in her breath at his harsh words. She should have been expecting it, but his threat, coming on the heels of their playful conversation and his generous actions, seemed even more evil.

"He's a good man," she said stiffly. "And if you think you're going to force him out without a fight, you're dead wrong. He's not the type to meekly shuffle away."

"I wonder if he knows what a loyal employee he has in you, Carly Ashton," Patrick mused aloud.

"I'm more than an employee."

"But you don't own equal shares. He could essentially let you go at any time by paying back your initial investment."

Carly took another calming drink of coffee. "So you've seen my contract. What of it?"

"You're not protected against a takeover or a reorganization, Carly. The guy stacked all the cards in his favor."

"I trust Bill," she retorted. Then slowly his words sank in. "If you're threatening to force me out, too, it won't work," she warned.

Patrick appeared unperturbed by her bristly tone. "Thinking of suing?"

Carly told herself that threatening to sue was the worst possible maneuver. It would only put Patrick on the defensive and cause him to maintain a harder line. The thing to do was to appeal to his sense of fair play.

Hah, she considered grimly, that was a good one. She'd yet to witness a hint of fairness in Patrick Ryan's corporate dealings. Well, she admitted, there was his willingness to share information with Bill. But that was just a drop in the bucket compared to everything else he had done.

"Of course I'm not," she denied calmly. "I was just considering my options." She didn't mention that one of them was to use Patrick's own plan against him. If she could rally support . . .

"Then consider this," he suggested. "I want you to stay on, Carly. Together we can make a go of it, if you'll only begin trusting me and stop fighting me at every turn."

Trust Patrick Ryan? The shark of Wall Street? The man must think he was dealing with Pollyanna.

"And Bill?"

The motion of his thrusting jaw suggested Patrick was grinding his teeth. "You're very loyal, aren't you?"

"So I've been told."

"Enough that I should consider you and McIntyre a package deal?" he inquired gruffly, as if anticipating the answer and disliking it immensely.

It only took Carly a split second to make a decision. "If Bill goes, I go," she agreed firmly.

Patrick muttered a soft oath and dragged his fingers through his hair as he rose from the desk and began pacing the room.

"Damn it, Carly, you've put me in an untenable position."

She held firm, meeting his blistering gaze with a steady one of her own. "That's the deal," she stated with amazing calm, considering the fact that giant condors were busily flapping their wings inside her stomach. "Take it or leave it."

Patrick turned away, staring out the window at the Washington Monument, a gleaming white monolith in the slate-gray sky. He should just take her up on it. Let her and her partner go to hell and take over Capitol himself, as he once would have.

"All right, I'll give you this one, Carly. But McIntyre doesn't have any say in the negotiations. Or the day-to-day running of Capitol until we have signed contracts from all the unions."

Carly shook her head. "He won't agree to that," she objected, wanting to salvage Bill's already damaged pride.

Patrick's gaze was firm. "I told you, Carly, he's already agreed to whatever's necessary. Including letting you go."

That hurt. But she wasn't as surprised as she might have been, given Bill's recent state of mind.

"You've made your point," she said softly. "Now may I make a suggestion?"

"Of course."

"There are a lot of wild rumors going around. I think you should meet with the employees and assure them that you're not the ogre they believe you to be."

"Ogre?" He appeared amused by the description. "That lovely young woman with the flaming red hair didn't seem to find me so threatening."

"Marge's only flaw is that she's far too susceptible to slippery masculine charm. I think it comes from growing up on a ranch with all those straight-talking cowboys." Carly's eyes narrowed. "I suppose you were on your best behavior."

Patrick answered with a broad, boyish grin. "Let's just say the senator would have been proud."

"Oh, no," Carly groaned. "We really need Marge to keep her mind on her work right now; she practically runs this place single-handedly. Why couldn't you have just been yourself?"

"Ouch," he complained. "That hurt, Carly."

The subject of their conversation suddenly appeared in the doorway. "Mr. Ryan?" Marge asked hesitantly.

Carly clenched her teeth as Patrick flashed a brilliant smile the secretary's way. "Yes, Marge?"

"I've worked up a tentative schedule for your meetings with the employees." She entered the room, handing Patrick a piece of paper.

"As you can see," Marge continued briskly, "I've broken everyone into groups. Secretarial, administrative, services, operations and computer personnel. I felt you might prefer this method. It will take more time, and you'll have to repeat yourself, but it also allows a more intimate setting."

Patrick studied the list. "It appears you've thought of everything, Marge. Thank you."

The woman smiled. "You're welcome. Shall I begin contacting people?"

Patrick nodded. "Please do." After Marge had left the room, he turned to Carly. "If that's what she's like when she's distracted, I'd love to see her at full throttle."

Seizing the moment, Carly ignored the slight stab of conscience she experienced for going behind Bill's back. "Marge is a marvel," she agreed enthusiastically. "I recommended that she be promoted into a management position in operations."

Patrick nodded. "With her organizational skills, that's the obvious place. What's she still doing working the desk?"

"Bill didn't want to lose her," Carly admitted softly.

Patrick glanced out the door of the office, watching Marge as she began to make the calls. "I can understand that," he said slowly. "And at this point in time, I have to admit that we could certainly use her right here. On the other hand, I hate to hold anyone back."

He tapped his fingers absently on the desktop as he considered the matter. "How about a compromise?" he suggested suddenly.

Carly could only nod. She was still having trouble accepting Patrick's fair appraisal of the situation. Whenever she was bound and determined to detest him, the man would switch gears on her and show a remarkably thoughtful side to his personality.

"What if we ask her to stay on until the negotiations are completed?" Patrick elaborated. "Then, among the three of us, we should be able to locate a secretary to take her place."

"I think that's a terrific idea," she agreed immediately. "That's very nice of you, Patrick."

"It's not nice at all," he countered abruptly. "It's simply intelligent management. It doesn't make any sense to waste talent."

Carly rose from the chair. "You're right, of course." As she reached the door she turned, the smile blooming openly on her face. "It was also very nice," she said as she left the office.

Carly was not at all surprised when later that morning Patrick managed to win over Capitol's employees, assuring them that for now, things would continue as usual. As Carly watched the waves of relief move across the nervous faces, she had to give Patrick credit for meeting with everybody.

"Of course, I'm sure it hasn't escaped your attention that Capitol is not as strong financially as we'd like," he admitted. He had his hands in his pockets, the gesture pushing his jacket back. "But we're not the only ones with that problem. Deregulation has forced everyone to make some adjustments. I promise that we'll do our best to come up with solutions that will protect as many jobs as possible. Also, personnel will be instructed to help anyone who might be displaced find new employment. The thing to remember is that we're all in this together."

He opened the floor to questions, and Carly was impressed as he seemed to know a great many of the employees by sight. He must have spent hours poring over the personnel files, she mused. That idea failed to give her peace of mind. If Patrick's intentions were to get Capitol back on its feet, then go on to his next challenge, why had he gone to the trouble of memorizing faces and names?

His answer, when she brought it up after the series of meetings sounded plausible.

"I've discovered that the larger the company, the more the employees appreciate being treated as individuals, so I had McIntyre get me copies of the personnel files when I agreed to take on this job. Let's face it, Carly, we're fighting an uphill battle here. We need all the troops behind us."

"Speaking of battles, are you going to let me in on what you're doing? Or is this a one-man show?"

Patrick shook his head regretfully. "I wish you'd trust me, Carly. It'd sure make all this a lot easier." He glanced down at his watch. "Why don't we send out for some sandwiches and we'll discuss it over lunch?"

Carly agreed and as they ate, Patrick began to unveil his master plan for the rescue of Capitol Airlines. She watched, entranced in spite of herself at the way his harsh features grew increasingly handsome as his enthusiasm accelerated. For the next three hours he seemed to have abandoned all interest in her as a woman, instead treating her as an equal partner as he outlined his scheme to allow Capitol's workers to buy into the company.

It was, she admitted secretly, a brilliant plan. The only problem was that it would take an equally brilliant individual to pull it off. Was Patrick Ryan that man?

Yes, Carly determined, Patrick Ryan would succeed at anything he put his mind to. In that respect, she knew she should be relieved that as the day wore on, he displayed no further interest in making love to her. But somehow, instead of being comforted by the lull in Patrick's seduction attempts, Carly found herself suffering from a vague sense of disappointment.

6

CARLY WAS STILL CONSIDERING her uncharacteristic attraction to Patrick when the intercom buzzed. When Marge informed him that his mother was on the line, Patrick muffled a soft oath.

"Hello." There was no warmth in the greeting and Carly rose, intending to give Patrick privacy. "No," he murmured, holding up his hand. "This won't take long."

Uncomfortable, but not wanting to precipitate another argument, Carly sat down again, pretending interest in the papers Patrick had given her to peruse.

"No, Mother," he stated on a deep sigh. "I wasn't talking to you. But I am busy, so if you could just get to the point."

Carly watched surreptitiously as a look of sheer frustration marched across Patrick's face.

"No, I don't think I can make it," he said firmly. "I told you when you called last week, I'm very involved right now. I don't have time for socializing."

Although Carly knew it was impolite to eavesdrop, it was impossible to miss the aggravation in Patrick's tone.

"I don't give a damn what the senator wants," he stated harshly, his fingers tightening around the receiver. "No, you can't come here . . . Because I'm up to my eyebrows in work."

Realizing that tenacity was a Ryan family trait, Carly was not surprised that his mother seemed to persist. Patrick closed his eyes and raked his fingers through his hair in frustration.

"Oh, hell, if it'll keep him from coming over to the office, tell the senator I'll be there."

Carly quickly returned her eyes to the papers in her lap as he hung up. She was taken aback when Patrick acted as though the conversation had never taken place.

"Okay," he stated briskly, "where were we?"

Carly was not able to refocus on business quite so abruptly. Her mind struggled to catch up with Patrick even as she wondered how he could instantly put aside what had obviously been a discomforting conversation. In fact, she considered, eyeing him warily, if anyone were to walk in right then, that person would never know that only a moment before Patrick had felt such ill will.

"I have to admit," Carly said, finally recalling what had been on her mind before the untimely interruption, "I'm worried about Bill. You're taking away all his decision-making powers with this new corporate structure."

Patrick pulled off the dark-framed glasses he used for reading and folded the stems back and forth as he appeared to give thoughtful consideration to her words.

"Do you honestly believe the man is capable of making a rational decision about anything these days?"

Carly's soft, rippling sigh said more than words ever could. "Things could change."

"And pigs will fly," Patrick muttered.

His uncaring tone caused Carly's hackles to rise. "Damn you, nobody's perfect. Not even the mighty Patrick Ryan."

"Point taken," he agreed carelessly. "And if by any major miracle McIntyre does manage to stop jet setting all over the country and take an active interest in the company, he can resume an active role in the running of Capitol Airlines."

He glared at her across the desk. "Damn it, Carly, I've already agreed to keep him on in a figurehead position, which is a lot more than I'd originally planned. Since we both know that altruistic gesture was due solely to your blasted stubbornness, why don't you just drop the subject? You've gotten what you wanted, but don't push your luck, lady."

Carly tossed her head as she shot him a narrow-eyed look. "You have the coldest heart of any man I've ever met, Patrick Ryan. It would take a blowtorch to warm you up to anything even resembling a human being!"

The moment the words escaped, Carly wished she could take them back. She waited, her heart in her throat, for Patrick to pick up on the obvious innuendo. But he surprised her by rising from the desk, moving over to the counter.

"Want a refill of your coffee?" he asked casually.

Carly could only stare at his back, unwilling to trust her unruly tongue.

When she didn't answer, he looked back questioningly over his shoulder. "Carly? More coffee?"

"No, thank you," she managed in a thin voice. "I'm fine."

You're a lot more than fine, Carly Ashton, Patrick considered grimly. Damn the woman, anyway. It had taken every ounce of his concentration to keep the topic on business. He had refused to acknowledge the softness of her smile when she had begun to get the drift of his plan, and he'd managed to ignore the dark violet of her eyes, as well as that damn perfume that could drive a man insane. He had just been congratulating himself on a brilliantly performed charade when she hit him with that provocative challenge. Oh, how he would have loved to pull her into his arms and demonstrate exactly how little it would take to make his body heat to explosive temperatures.

But remembering that it was important they work together, he avoided her tender trap, pretending interest in another cup of coffee when what he really wanted was to lock the door and ravish her in every conceivable manner. And a few inconceivable ones, as well.

"So," he said as he flung his body back into the chair, "you've gotten what you wanted for good old Bill. Why keep harping on it?"

Carly was grateful for his uncaring attitude. It helped her remember that to get emotionally involved with this man would be a fatal mistake. She took a sip of her lukewarm coffee.

"I can't believe a hotshot executive like yourself hasn't read all the studies on what happens to individuals who find themselves suddenly put out to pasture."

"McIntyre's still going to have a place on the board, Carly. And he's been offered a helluva lot for his shares in Capitol. That money will buy a pretty piece of pasture."

Anger filled her eyes. "That's not what we're talking about and you know it!"

Patrick eyed her curiously. "Why are you shouting?"

"I'm *not* shouting!"

He braced his elbows on the desk as he continued to study her thoughtfully. "It sure sounds like shouting to me. A few notes up the scale and you'll shatter every window in this building."

"Damn it," she blazed furiously, "this isn't funny."

"I never said it was."

Her hands were trembling as she waved away his words. "Then don't joke about it!"

"I wasn't," he countered softly, restraining his own temper. If Carly had known Patrick Ryan better, she would have realized he was at his most dangerous when employing that silky smooth tone. "In fact, if you want to know the truth, I've never considered McIntyre a joking matter." His eyes hardened to chips of ice. "Tell me, Carly Ashton, does the man know how much you love him?"

Carly stared in simple disbelief. "What did you say?"

Patrick rose to stand over her, his stance meant to intimidate. "I asked," he repeated in a deceptively mild tone, "if you've let McIntyre know your true feelings." His gaze raked over her suddenly pale features. "Is that why he invited you to buy in, Carly? Are you and McIntyre partners in the most—" he cleared his throat and arched an insinuating brow "—intimate sense of the word?"

Overcome with blinding fury, Carly jumped up, her eyes blazing with righteous anger. "That's disgusting," she ground out. "You have absolutely no right to even suggest for a moment that I . . . that Bill and I—"

"Carly," Patrick cut her off smoothly, "do you or do you not love the guy?"

His voice was calm and controlled, but his eyes were alive with a dangerous intensity that took her breath away. She backed up a few steps. "That's a complicated question," she complained in a trembling undertone.

Patrick moved toward her, closing the slight gap. "Try giving me a simple answer," he suggested. Although he still had not raised his voice, Carly recognized the request for what it was. A command. Softly couched, but written in stone.

Carly ran an agitated hand through her hair. "I do love Bill," she insisted, raising her chin in silent defiance to the anger that suddenly flashed in Patrick's eyes. "Just as I love his wife. And his daughter."

At the thought of beautiful Meredith and the valiant fight she had been putting up these past two years, Carly felt all fight drain out of her. She slumped back into her chair, folding her arms on the desk, lowering her head to them.

"Please just leave me alone, Patrick," she murmured on a low, flat note.

The slight stab of guilt Patrick experienced for upsetting Carly was overshadowed by his relief that she wasn't having an affair with McIntyre. He reached down, his fingers kneading the tense muscles of her shoulders.

"Carly..."

"Leave me alone," she repeated, her words muffled.

Patrick squatted beside her, lifting her unwilling gaze to his. "I was out of line," he admitted. "But I could tell you were hiding something about the guy, and for Capitol's sake I had to know if you and McIntyre were more than business partners."

That was not exactly true, but Patrick wasn't prepared to admit how much of that information was required for his own peace of mind.

Carly frowned. "I'm not the type of woman to have affairs with married men."

Actually she wasn't the type of woman to have affairs, period, Patrick decided. He had no illusions that Carly was, at thirty-one, still a virgin. Yet he knew that for her to go to bed with a man, there would have to be a strong emotional bond. He was crazy to even be considering the prospect of making love to her. But Lord, how he wanted her!

"I believe you," he said simply. "Are you sure you don't want to talk about what's bothering you?"

"Positive," Carly insisted. While that was not quite true, she didn't want to share such intimate feelings with Patrick. Those vivid blue eyes saw far too much as it was.

He stifled his irritation. She was keeping something from him. Something important. That idea was in direct contradiction with Carly's usual behavior. He couldn't remember ever meeting such a forthright individual.

"Well, then," he stated conversationally, "I suppose we'd better get back to work. This is no way to run a railroad. Or in our case, an airline."

Or a relationship, Carly added silently as Patrick once again put the desk between them. She wisely refrained from stating her thoughts aloud, instead returning to the subject of the union negotiations.

"So," she said, tapping her pen on the yellow legal pad, "we have two weeks to tender an acceptable offer."

"That's about it," he agreed, taking a drink of coffee.

Patrick watched a line furrow on her brow as she reread the union's ultimatum. "If they're willing to give us this time, why didn't they just postpone the vote until we made them an offer?"

"They already had an offer, Carly," he reminded her. "The problem was, Capitol's offer was totally one-sided. I don't know what McIntyre thought he was accomplishing with that proposal."

"It was the best we could do," she murmured, unwilling to stab her friend in the back by telling Patrick about the arguments she'd raised along those very lines.

"Did you really think they'd go for a twenty percent cut in wages and benefits?" he asked incredulously.

Carly brushed back her bangs with a frustrated gesture. "Of course I didn't," she retorted.

Patrick softened his tone. "You can't grab with both hands, Carly. We have to give something with the right hand if we're taking away with the left."

"You're right. . . . But it still seems to me they could have been reasonable and postponed the vote."

He brushed off her concern. "It was simply a power play; don't worry about it. I don't expect any problems when I meet with Clayton this afternoon to table the new offer. Believe me, the machinists are the least of our concerns."

She lifted her head from the papers, studying him curiously. "What do you know that you're not telling me?"

"I can deal with Clayton," he said, swiveling thoughtfully in his chair. "He's a strong leader and the machinists are, admittedly, a fairly militant union. But they're also pragmatists, who can spot an honest, fair deal when they see one."

"If it's that simple, why do I detect a 'but' in your answer?"

He pulled off the glasses again, staring out the window. The snow had stopped falling sometime during the night, and the winter day had dawned bright and clear. The sun was as bright as Carly's yellow sweater, which reminded him of her slender, but decidedly feminine, body under that bright wool. He found himself smiling, despite the seriousness of their situation.

"Patrick?" Carly's soft voice shattered his pleasant reverie and he sighed.

"The flight attendants will take their cue from the machinists. It's the pilots who could end up being the fly in the ointment."

"The pilots?" Carly repeated. "But they have the weakest union of the three."

"That's precisely the problem. The union is too decentralized to ensure a quick decision."

Carly chewed thoughtfully on a fingernail, obviously considering Patrick's words. When she lifted her gaze, Patrick was once again entranced by the intelligence sparking those lovely, dark eyes.

"If they're so decentralized," she said slowly, "it'll be harder to convince them to yield any power."

He rewarded her with a broad grin. "Exactly." Then his face returned to its previous cautionary expression. "They've got a twenty-man board and at least two of the members of that board are less than appreciative of management's position."

Carly gave him a clear, candid look. "You'll turn them around."

"Good Lord, is that actually a vote of confidence?"

She flicked her hair back over her shoulder. "I'm discovering that there are a few advantages to having a shark on my side."

"You're a hard woman, Ms Ashton."

"Hard to get," she agreed, rising to her feet. "Well, if I'm not mistaken, you're meeting with the machinists' representatives in twenty minutes. I don't suppose you'll be back this afternoon?"

"Probably not. Would you like to have dinner after my meeting? We can discuss the outcome."

"Sorry. I've got a dance class tonight."

"Capitol Airlines is hovering on the brink of disaster and you're going out tap-dancing?"

Carly laughed. "Good try, Patrick, but I don't succumb to guilt. You've already assured me you don't expect any problems, and we both know that the ball is in your court. So go out and hit an ace for the home team. If anything unexpected happens, call me. Otherwise, I'll see you in the morning."

Patrick watched the smooth swing of her hips as she left his office. It wasn't going to be as easy as he'd first thought, he considered as he stuffed the papers into his ancient leather briefcase. Carly was a forthright individual. He doubted that she possessed a talent for duplicity or prevarication. If he came right out and asked, she'd probably admit that she was as attracted to him as he was to her.

But Patrick was beginning to realize it wasn't that simple. Carly Ashton was one of those fortunate individuals who honestly liked herself. Not that she was conceited or egotistical, but she was well aware of her self-worth. Alex had stated Carly deserved better than what Patrick had to offer. Carly, it appeared, concurred.

Exhaling a deep breath, he put on his coat and left the office, vowing to put the exasperating woman from his mind.

* * *

SIX HOURS LATER, Patrick was forced to admit the impossibility of that decision. When he showed up at Alex's front door, his old friend did not appear at all surprised to see him.

"I had a call from Carly this evening," Alex stated, handing Patrick a glass of imported cognac.

Patrick feigned disinterest. "So?"

"That's right, you're not interested in her personally," Alex recalled. "Only professionally." He settled into an antique Hepplewhite chair, crossing his legs, his dark eyes dancing. "So we won't waste time talking about her. Shall we discuss instead the latest in the ongoing campaign to return a Ryan to the senate?"

"I figured you'd be invited to that party," Patrick muttered.

Alex grinned. "Of course. An extra man is a valuable asset at any party in Washington. By remaining single I eat at all the best homes, drink the finest imported wines and pick up the highest level gossip."

"Speaking of gossip, you were right about the senator's decision to retire," Patrick said. "The problem is, he isn't ready to give up politics completely."

"If I recall correctly, you were struggling to avoid your father's plans to bring you into the political arena when we first met. I suppose this latest decision has renewed the senator's determination?"

"You've called that one right," Patrick agreed. "As it turns out, this is the worst possible time for me to have come to Washington. At least in Manhattan I was less accessible to the old man's manipulations."

"I can't see you being manipulated into anything you didn't want to do."

"Of course not. But I've got enough to worry about without trying to dodge the senator's little snares.... What did she want?"

Alex stroked his black mustache thoughtfully. "I assume we're back to Carly."

Patrick leaned forward, his forearms braced on his thighs. "Did she ask about me?"

Alex arched a midnight-black brow. "You? Why would she care to discuss your business relationship with me?"

"Damn it, Alex, stop playing games. She's driving me up a wall, and I want to know what she said to you."

Alex's eyes narrowed. "Are you asking me to betray a confidence? Carly's my friend, Patrick."

"You were my friend first!"

Alex laughed, shaking his head. "You remind me of an *I Love Lucy* rerun. Lucy feels left out when Ethel's old high school chum comes to town for a visit."

Patrick managed a slight self-deprecating smile. "I told you she was making me crazy."

"Carly has that effect on people," Alex agreed amiably. "Her candor is unnerving. Especially to such confirmed bachelors as you and I, who are used to spending our energies avoiding more cunning feminine ploys."

"I don't know," Patrick considered. "I think it's possible that Carly's little tricks are far more fatal."

"They're not tricks."

Patrick tossed off the rest of the cognac. "I know," he muttered. "That's precisely why they're so dangerous."

"You're attracted to her."

"Who wouldn't be?"

Alex eyed his friend thoughtfully. "But I believe it's more than that. You're beginning to care for her, aren't you?"

"Don't be ridiculous. She's just another woman. And a skinny one at that."

"No, you're wrong," he argued. "Carly is far more than just another woman. She's special. And she's more vulnerable than she seems, Patrick."

"Are you kidding? The woman is tough as nails. She's been fighting me every step of the way on the Capitol reorganization."

"That doesn't sound like her," Alex commented. "Despite her appearing charmingly disorganized, Carly has quite a good business head on her shoulders."

"I realize that. But she keeps setting up roadblocks with her stubborn loyalty to McIntyre."

Alex leaned back in his chair, his gaze direct. "I've always considered loyalty an asset. There was a time when you felt the same way."

Patrick knew they were talking about Julia once again. "I don't want to talk about my marriage," he insisted, his mouth a taut, grim slash.

"It was a good marriage, Patrick," Alex reminded him needlessly.

"And now it's over. Let's just drop it, all right?"

Alex shook his head regretfully. "You didn't fail her, my friend. You did all that was humanly possible."

Patrick's expression hardened to granite. "She still died."

Alex expelled a frustrated breath. "Do you want another drink?" he asked, rising from his chair to refill his own glass.

Patrick shook his head. A heavy silence hung between the two men. A silence Alex eventually broke.

"You have always been too successful for your own good," he gently accused.

"What does that mean?"

"It means that you don't know how to lose. When faced with a problem, you put your head down and forge full steam ahead. It's a 'damn the torpedoes' mentality that usually works quite well. The problem is that every so often, even the strongest man must realize that certain things are beyond his control."

Alex had hit a little too close to home for comfort. Patrick chose not to answer.

"Julia's death was a tragic thing, Patrick," Alex continued softly. "But you can't continue to avoid personal entanglements simply because you find yourself unable to completely control events. You must open your heart to what life has to offer; take things as they come. It's time for you to think of marrying again."

"That's terrific advice, coming from one of Washington's most infamous bachelors," Patrick ground out. "When was the last time you had a relationship that lasted any longer than the usual campaign promise?"

"Believe me," Alex countered soberly, "if I ever met a woman capable of messing up my mind the way Carly Ashton has done to you, I would move heaven and earth to marry her."

Patrick pushed himself out of the chair, putting his glass on the table. "That's an intriguing scenario; I just hope I'm around when it happens. I'd love a front row seat to watch you make a fool of yourself."

"You'll be the first to know," Alex replied cheerfully, putting his arm around Patrick's shoulders as he walked him to the door. "In the meantime, I shall have to make the most of my lonely bachelor's existence."

That drew an appreciative laugh. "Speaking of lonely," Patrick stated, "I have to admit I was surprised to find you home alone."

Alex grinned. "As it so happens, my companion for the evening is a legislative aide to your father. The senator is planning a filibuster before the budget vote to protest social cuts. Marianne had to work late, gathering up appropriate reading material."

As Patrick left the house, a taxi pulled up to the curb. A tall, shapely brunette exited with a show of long leg, smiling past him toward Alex, who was standing in the doorway.

"My heart bleeds for you," Patrick called back over his shoulder. Alex simply laughed as he waved goodbye.

As Patrick walked to his car, he realized that coming here had proved fruitless; he was as confused as ever. The only thing he was sure about was that he was getting sick and tired of Alex's warnings. Carly was a grown woman and Patrick had not offered anything more than he was capable of giving. When she came to him—and Patrick had no doubt that she would—Carly would know precisely what she was getting into. How many women could say that?

So why did he feel so lousy about the idea? The answer to that question remained elusive as Patrick drove back to Georgetown.

7

WHEN CARLY ARRIVED at Capitol Airlines' offices the next morning, she was not surprised to find Patrick already at work.

"I like that dress," he stated as she entered his office. His gaze lingered over slender curves enhanced by the scarlet sweater dress. "Although how you expect me to keep my mind on work today, I'll never know. A man could get arrested for the ideas that little number inspires."

Carly refused to blush at the gleam in his eyes. "I'm going straight to the concert from here."

He braced his elbows on the arms of the chair, steepling his fingers together. "Ah, yes, the concert. With my dear old friend Alex. I envy him."

Patrick's tone, as well as his expression, remained inscrutable, but Carly felt a sudden renewed tension in the air. "Perhaps I should cancel. What with all the problems around here—"

"Don't worry about it," he cut in abruptly. "While I'm admittedly more of a workaholic than our absent friend McIntyre, I'm not a slave driver, Carly."

"If you're sure," she responded hesitantly.

"I'm sure."

Carly glanced over at the coffeepot. It was already nearly empty, revealing that he had begun work very early.

"Let me get us both a cup of coffee and you can tell me about your success with Clayton," she suggested.

She was almost out the door when Patrick called to her. "Carly?"

She turned back toward him. "Yes?"

"How do you know my lobbying was successful?"

Carly had already dropped her plan to steal the reins of power back from Patrick. It was obvious that the rumors about him were either exaggerated or dated. As far as she could tell, Patrick had no intention of absconding with Capitol for his own gains, so she had decided to stay on and help him save the company. The grin she now flashed was sincere.

"Because, Patrick Ryan, I can't imagine you being anything else."

He smiled at that, putting his glasses back on as he returned to his paperwork. Despite the myriad problems he faced this morning, Carly's words left him unreasonably lighthearted.

As she made her way to Capitol's lunchroom, Carly found herself vaguely wishing that Patrick had asked her to give up the concert this evening. *That's ridiculous*, she scolded herself. *The thing to do is to get out before you find yourself in over your head.* Despite every ounce of common sense she possessed, it was impossible not to admit she found Patrick Ryan far too appealing for her own good.

By the time she returned to the office with their coffee, Carly had forced her mind back to Capitol's business problems.

"It's an acceptable compromise," she stated after Patrick told her that though Clayton had not promised anything at yesterday's meeting, the indications were that the machinists would agree to the latest offer. "They'd be crazy to turn it down."

"We're in agreement there. Now, about the pilots—" The blare of the intercom interrupted his intended statement.

"Yes, Marge?"

"Mr. McIntyre on line one," the secretary's disembodied voice offered tentatively. "For Ms Ashton."

"Is it a local call?" Patrick asked.

"No, sir, he's calling from Stowe, Vermont."

"I'll take it." Patrick picked up the receiver before Carly could reach it. "McIntyre," he stated brusquely, "I suppose you're calling about the machinists."

Carly glared at him as she held her hand out for the receiver. Patrick turned the chair, steadfastly ignoring her. "What the hell do you mean, we can talk about that later? It's precisely that attitude that got Capitol into trouble in the first place."

Patrick's face was etched with grim, angry lines as he thrust the receiver toward an equally furious Carly. "He wants to talk to you."

"I'll take it in my office."

"You'll take it here."

"The hell I will," she snapped, marching from the room in long, angry strides.

Patrick watched her go in stunned silence. Tersely he transferred the call, then slammed the receiver down with unnecessary force.

He was standing at the window, his hands jammed into the pockets of his navy suit when Carly returned.

"Bill appreciates your efforts," she said, her words directed at his broad back.

Patrick didn't turn around. "You've no idea what a relief that is," he said sarcastically.

"Let's not fight," Carly requested softly. "We were getting along so well."

"What could you have to say to McIntyre that you couldn't say in front of me?" he asked, his gaze still directed out the window.

Carly sighed, coming across the plush expanse of carpeting to stand behind him. "Are you by any chance jealous of Bill?"

Patrick didn't answer immediately, drowning in her soft scent. He told himself that these feelings that had been driving him insane were nothing more than simple desire for Carly. It had to be that. Because there was no room in his life for anything else.

"I just don't think this is any time for us to be keeping secrets from each other," he muttered.

He was a fine one to talk, Carly considered with a burst of anger. He'd been keeping something far more important from her since the beginning. She sensed it every time it seemed that Patrick might admit some honest emotion toward her. She vowed to spend the evening badgering Alex until he gave in and revealed what was going on in his old friend's mind.

"Bill is in Vermont visiting his daughter," Carly said quietly. "She's in a rehabilitation clinic there. It's really more of a resort than a hospital. The building is a lovely old New England inn surrounded by woods. There's a lake and plenty of room for the patients, uh, the residents to walk and relax. Those who can walk, that is."

Patrick slowly turned around, watching Carly as she ran her finger over her great-grandmother's wedding band.

"How long has she been there?"

"Two months."

"And before that?"

"She's been in six hospitals over the past two years."

"About the time McIntyre started neglecting his duties at Capitol."

Carly nodded, closing her eyes momentarily against the flood of pain that swept over her.

"What's she doing there, Carly?"

When she opened her eyes, the pain Patrick viewed in their depths wrenched at something deep inside him. "Meredith was my roommate in college," she stated slowly. "We were like sisters."

"That's how you met McIntyre?"

She nodded, tears brightening her eyes. Patrick watched with admiration as she fought them back. "Gramps died my senior year in high school and I felt so alone. So lost." She looked up at this man who behaved as if he'd never experienced such emotions. "Can you possibly understand how miserable I was?"

"I can," Patrick agreed roughly.

Carly studied him thoughtfully for a moment, but his gaze was suddenly expertly shielded, so she continued. "The day I moved into my dorm room, Meredith showed up with Bill and Elaine. They were so friendly, so loving, I felt as if I was a member of the family."

"What happened to her?"

Carly was staring past him, out the window, but Patrick had the feeling Carly was not seeing the crisp February day. "After college, we stayed close. Two years ago, we had planned a ski trip for the last weekend of the season, but I came down with a cold and didn't go. Bill was driving, and a drunk driver..."

A lump rose in her throat and Carly could only shake her head, closing her eyes against the scene she'd imagined far too many times. As Patrick wrapped his arms around her, she allowed herself to lean against him, drawing from his strength, receiving comfort to the lingering sense of guilt she'd never been able to express.

"Thank God you didn't go." His voice was unusually husky.

Carly lifted her gaze to his. "I've always felt a little guilty about that."

"Don't," he commanded. "You couldn't have changed anything, Carly. All you could have done is end up in that hospital yourself. Or dead." At that thought, Patrick's arms tightened about her.

Fearing that he was about to crush her ribs, Carly pushed tentatively against his chest. "Patrick . . ."

He forced himself to let her go. "Sorry," he muttered, instructing his heart to slow down.

Carly took a deep breath. "Meredith suffered a severe injury to her spine. The doctors all said she'd never walk again. Bill refused to believe that, and he's spent the past two years taking her all over the world to specialists."

Her expression softened. "He called to tell me that she's shown some improvement," Carly related, her palms pressed tightly together. "They're hoping this time there'll be a real breakthrough."

As he watched the unmistakable spark gleam in her eyes, Patrick had to bite down the advice that Carly shouldn't allow herself to hope for the impossible. He knew how such irrational hope could bring additional pain.

"I hope so, too," he agreed softly.

Their eyes held, exchanging a series of intimate messages. Carly was relieved, but a little disappointed when the brisk businessman returned to take the place of a surprisingly sympathetic individual.

"Ready to get back to work?"

Carly inclined her head. "Ready. . . Thank you, Patrick," she stated suddenly. "I've kept my feelings about the accident to myself, because I didn't want to burden Bill. But I'll admit to needing a little TLC just then."

He gave her a slow, considering smile. "Anytime, Carly. Anytime at all."

The silent truce remained in effect throughout the morning. When Patrick offered to take Carly out to lunch, she declined, assuring him the yogurt she had brought from home was sufficient. Patrick ordered a hamburger from the deli down the street and they worked through the lunch hour once again, formulating their negotiating strategy for the pilots' union.

"It's an excellent offer," Carly stated, stirring the blueberries through the smooth, creamy yogurt. "They'd be crazy to turn it down." As she licked the spoon, Patrick was hit with a jolt of the desire he'd kept carefully banked all morning.

"Agreed. Do you have to eat that stuff?" he asked weakly.

Carly looked at him in surprise. "I like it. And at least it isn't crawling off the plate." She eyed his rare hamburger with obvious disdain. "And look at those french fries."

He glanced down at the cardboard box. "What's wrong with my french fries?"

She reached out, holding one up between her fingers. "They're dripping with grease," she pointed out. "Do you have any idea how much cholesterol is in one of these things?"

"No." He held up a hand as she opened her mouth to tell him. "And I don't want to know. I happen to like greasy rare hamburgers and soggy french fries, okay?"

"Of course, Patrick," she agreed sweetly. "You're entitled to eat anything you like. Even if it is junk food."

He grinned. "One man's junk . . ." he stated, popping a catsup-drenched french fry into his mouth.

Although Carly struggled to concentrate on their negotiating tactics the remainder of the afternoon, their proximity kept drawing her mind to more stimulating thoughts. She knew that though he kept the conversation on business matters, Patrick was sharing her thoughts. Too many times their eyes had met over the top of the desk and held for just a heartbeat before dropping back to the stacks of papers.

Patrick was still immersed in paperwork when she left, and even if she was looking forward to this evening, some part of her secretly wished for an excuse to remain at the office.

Alex had agreed to meet her outside the Lisner Auditorium at George Washington University, and Carly was relieved when he was prompt, as usual. The temperature had dropped, and though the sky was clear, the wind stung her cheeks.

"Why didn't I stay in Florida?" she complained, rubbing her hands together as they made their way to their seats.

"And I in Cairo," he agreed. "I thought Washington was supposed to have a mild climate."

"They've been having a blizzard in Vermont," Carly remarked.

His dark face split in a broad, accepting grin. "Then I suppose we should be grateful for what we have."

"Absolutely," she answered. "Besides, last I heard, Mangione had yet to play Cairo."

"Speaking of which," Alex stated conversationally, "do you still possess that burning desire to see my homeland?"

To Carly, Egypt had always seemed one of the most mysterious, romantic spots on the face of the earth. Others could have Paris's Champs-Elysées or Venice's canals. If she could have one glimpse of the pyramids, she'd die a happy woman.

"You know I do. Why?"

"Because I'm going back next month."

Carly's happy face fell. "Oh. I'm going to miss you," she said sadly.

Alex laughed, his body shaking with his pleasure. "You have the most expressive face, Carly. It is a delight to read so clearly what is in your heart." He lifted her hand to his lips. "Most American women guard their secrets much better."

"I'm working on it," she mumbled, disliking the idea that Patrick might be able to read what went on in her head whenever she looked at him.

Alex chucked her under the chin. "Well, cheer up, my lovely. Because I am only returning home for a short time. Two, perhaps three, weeks. And I'd like very much for you to accompany me."

Carly stared at him. "Come with you? Why?"

His expression was suddenly sly. "Can't I invite you on a little vacation?" he asked blandly.

She shook her head, flicking her hair back over her shoulder. "Come on, Alex. I'm not the usual type of woman you invite on your little junkets."

"Not you, too," he protested, his smile belying his affronted tone. "I've had two such discussions with Patrick lately. He dared to accuse me of being a hit-and-run artist."

Even hearing the man's name affects me, Carly considered wonderingly as that now familiar warmth flooded through her. She managed a teasing smile as she patted Alex's cheek.

"If the shoe fits," she murmured. "Now tell me what precipitated this intriguing invitation."

At that precise moment the houselights dimmed and Alex turned his attention to the stage. "Later," he promised. "During supper."

Even the brilliance of Chuck Mangione could not keep Carly's mind from wandering to Patrick. What was he doing? Was he with some other woman? Had they already shared a candlelit dinner and returned to the house for a long, romantic evening?

Knock it off, she told herself firmly, forcing her mind back to the swelling sounds of the flügelhorn. Talk about hit and run—Patrick Ryan had elevated the concept of casual sex to an Olympian sport. He even had rules, for pete's sake!

Alex was happily humming off-key as they left the auditorium for a late-night supper club. Carly waited until their drinks had been delivered before returning to the subject of his trip.

"Why do you want me to go to Egypt?" she asked, plucking the olive from her martini.

Alex didn't answer immediately. Instead he took a sip of icy Russian vodka. "Ah, that's nice," he said, sighing happily. "I'm so glad your country is no longer boycotting the real thing."

"Alex," Carly prompted. "You're avoiding my question."

"It's my family," he revealed. "Specifically my mother."

"Your mother," Carly repeated blankly.

"Yes... You see, Carly, I really am homesick, but every time I return to Cairo, my mother parades a constant string of eligible women in front of me. So help me, every time I go home, I'm made to feel like a perpetual contestant on *The Dating Game*."

"So tell her you're not interested."

Alex expelled a weary sigh. "It's obvious you have never met my mother."

"Even so, what do your family problems have to do with me?" she asked. Then slowly comprehension began to dawn. "Oh, no," Carly stated firmly. "I'm not going to Cairo to help you trick your mother."

Alex reached across the table, clasping her hands in his. "Carly, be reasonable. I'm offering you an all-expense-paid vacation to the country of your dreams."

"I won't do it," she insisted.

His dark eyes turned to melted chocolates. "Don't think of it as chicanery," he coaxed. "Instead, believe that you'd be making a poor old Egyptian woman very happy."

"If I remember correctly, your mother isn't Egyptian. She's American," Carly countered.

Alex appeared unperturbed by Carly's objection. "Egyptian, American, what does it matter? She's a mother, Carly. And the one universal truth is that all mothers, regardless of nationality, wish nothing more than to see their sons happily married. You can make that wish come true, Carly."

"Now we're getting married?"

"Of course not. We're just going to tell her that we're engaged."

"And then?" she asked suspiciously.

Alex shrugged. "We will return to America for a long engagement. My mother is not a young woman; who knows how long she has left in this world? All we'd have to do would be to keep up the charade in a few letters. A phone call once in a while."

Carly felt herself weakening and hated herself for succumbing to those liquid dark eyes and that pitiful story about his aged mother.

"Damn you, Alex," she muttered. "It's a stupid idea and it couldn't possibly work."

"But you'll think about it," he said, reading her expression.

"I'll think about it," she agreed reluctantly.

He lifted his glass toward her in a toast. "You're a wonderful woman, Carly. If by any chance I ever wished to marry, you'd be my very first choice."

She grimaced at the backhanded compliment. "Thanks loads." Then she linked her fingers under her chin and gave him a look. "There's a price," she warned.

He waved away her concern. "I will pay for everything."

Carly shook her head. "No, this is something else. A personal favor."

"Anything," Alex replied expansively. "I spare no expense when it comes to my mother's happiness."

"Tell me about Patrick. About whatever it is that has him so afraid of commitment."

Alex immediately dropped his gaze, his dark eyes intent on a nonexistent spot on his silverware. "I don't know what you mean," he mumbled.

Carly reached across the table, covering his hand as he fiddled nervously with his cutlery. "Alex, it's a fair trade. Relief from your mother for a little information about Patrick Ryan."

His eyes darted to her face. "Then you'll come with me?"

Knowing that it was the worst possible time to be leaving the country, Carly nodded slowly. Whatever happened to Capitol, she knew instinctively that Alex held the key to her future.

"I'll go," she agreed. "Now talk, Alex."

His eyes circled the room, as if seeking out spies, then lowering his voice, he told her everything. From the day he'd first met Patrick, Patrick's marriage to the lovely English girl, and the long, lingering months that Patrick was forced to sit by helplessly as his wife fought a losing battle against leukemia.

"He loved her very much, didn't he?" she asked softly.

"He adored her," Alex agreed. "And she him."

He studied her thoughtfully, as if carefully weighing his words. "I believe Patrick has very strong feelings for you, Carly. But whether he will admit to such feelings . . ." He shrugged helplessly.

"Why is he so reluctant?"

Alex sighed. "Patrick is a man who insists on being in control at all times. Surely you've witnessed that while working with him."

Carly nodded.

"Julia's illness took that control away from him. For the first few months he refused to believe she was dying. He dragged her from one clinic to another, ignoring his work. Finding a cure became an obsession with him."

Carly immediately thought of Bill's refusal to accept Meredith's prognosis. "I can understand that," she murmured.

Alex sipped his drink. "Actually, there was an odd reversal of roles in their marriage. I had always considered Julia the soft one; she never made demands, never raised her voice. She was probably one of the most gentle women I have ever met."

Carly squashed the burst of envy that entered her mind. What type of woman was she, feeling that way toward someone who had suffered such an unhappy end to her life? With her characteristic lack of self-deception, Carly admitted that no one would ever describe her as acquiescent or gentle. It was that thought that had caused the unruly jealousy; she didn't like the idea of Patrick comparing her to his perfect wife and finding her wanting.

"You said there was a role reversal?" she asked quietly.

"Patrick had always appeared to be the rock of their relationship, but it was Julia who had the strength to rise to the occasion," Alex explained. "When Patrick arranged a trip to Tijuana, to enroll her in some back-roads clinic specializing in a treatment featuring rose hips or citrus seeds or some such nonsense, she put her foot down, insisting on the right to die peacefully."

Carly's breath caught in her throat. "What did he do then?"

Alex's dark eyes were grave. "He took her home and stayed with her that last month. Surprisingly enough, Julia seemed happier during those days than she had been the entire two years. It was hard on Patrick, but he had never been able to deny her anything. After her death, he threw himself into his work. You know the rest."

"She must have been an incredible lady."

"She was that," Alex agreed.

"I can understand why Patrick has no intention of getting emotionally involved again." Carly managed a crooked smile. "Julia sounds like a tough act for any woman to follow." Her fingers gathered the tablecloth into nervous folds.

"You've got it all wrong," Alex objected. "I believe Patrick refuses to let himself care for anyone because love isn't something you can control." He studied Carly thoughtfully. "As you've already discovered for yourself."

Carly immediately ducked behind the menu, pretending intense interest in the listed fare. "I don't know what you're talking about."

"Of course you do," Alex countered. "But I won't bother to argue such an obvious point. Have you tried the scampi here? It's quite good."

They took a few minutes to order, Carly vacillating between the scampi and the veal piccata. Taking Alex's advice, she settled on the scampi. She was relieved when the dinner conversation turned to the more usual subject of politics. Senator Ryan had begun his filibuster, as promised, reading selected excerpts from *Oliver Twist* and *A Tale of Two Cities* to a nearly deserted senate chamber.

"It's too bad that it's February," Carly said. "A couple months ago he could have packed the house by reading *A Christmas Carol* during the holiday season."

"He chose Dickens to symbolize the suffering of the poor," Alex enlightened her.

Carly looked at him curiously. "How on earth do you know that?"

"I happen to know the lady who selected the appropriate passages."

Carly laughed. "I do hope you're planning to leave your body to science, Alex. The medical report should be an instant bestseller."

Alex grimaced. "You sound as if you've been rehearsing those accusations with Patrick. Believe me, my reputation with the ladies is highly exaggerated." He flashed her a brilliant smile. "However, since it seems to garner me a surfeit of party invitations, who am I to disillusion people?"

"Who indeed?" Carly sighed, leaning back in her chair. "That was delicious, Alex. Thank you."

"Thank *you*," he answered. "I can't remember when I've enjoyed an evening more."

"Mangione was marvelous, wasn't he?"

"Superb," Alex agreed. "But I was referring to the company." When she appeared disconcerted, he began to laugh. "Don't misunderstand me," he protested, holding up his hand. "I've always found you delightful company, Carly. But I have no intention of complicating your life further than my old friend already has. It was just a relief not to have to worry about impressing you with my sparkling repartee."

Carly's eyes were filled with reluctant laughter. "I think I'll take that as a compliment."

"Please do."

Her expression sobered. "You know, Alex, you should give some thought to settling down."

He appeared honestly horrified by her suggestion. "I swear you and Patrick are involved in a conspiracy to get me married off."

"Would that be so bad?"

"I believe this is the time to plead the Fifth Amendment," he stated laughingly. Then his smiling expression turned grave. "I wish you the best, Carly. You know that, don't you?"

She stood, plucking her cape from the back of the chair. "I do," she agreed softly. "Just as I know you're a big fake."

A black brow climbed his forehead. "Me? A fake?" He flung his hand against his chest as he rose from the table to stand beside her.

"A fake," Carly repeated firmly. "Inside that world-weary exterior beats the heart of an incurable romantic," she accused with a soft smile, going up on her toes to press a quick kiss against his cheek.

"Let me know how everything turns out," Alex instructed as he walked her to her car.

But Carly failed to hear him; her mind was occupied with thoughts of Patrick.

8

As PATRICK SAT ALONE in the dark, he couldn't stop wondering what Carly and his old friend were doing now. He should have insisted she work overtime this evening, he considered darkly. That would have kept her out of the hands of that Middle Eastern Casanova. Despite his friendship with Alex, despite his firm conviction that Carly did not indulge in casual sex, Patrick found himself irrationally, furiously, jealous.

Unused to such tumultuous emotions, he sought to solve the puzzle that was Carly Ashton. There were times in her company when he felt more relaxed and at ease than he had with any other person. Including Julia, he admitted reluctantly. Julia had been like a hothouse orchid; she had needed someone to care for her. Not that he'd minded. From the moment they'd said their vows, Patrick had realized that his bride had put her life in his hands. It had made him feel proud to be worthy of such trust.

Carly, on the other hand, obviously preferred to make her own decisions, to forge her own path. Patrick couldn't remember ever meeting anyone so self-sufficient. Unless it was himself, he conceded. One trait he and Carly shared in spades was their independence. Other than that, they had next to nothing in common.

While Patrick enjoyed the challenge of his work, his analytical method of solving a problem was a direct contrast to Carly's impulsive behavior that often defied logic. Yet, he admitted the end results were the same. From what he could tell, Carly would succeed in whatever project she undertook. Patrick chalked up yet another attribute in common, surprised that he had discovered even two.

He sipped a glass of Scotch as he continued to consider the effect Carly had on his well-ordered life. Just as he found himself able to relax in her presence, there were other times when he found her unreasonably distracting. Disturbing. Of course he wanted her; what man in his right mind wouldn't?

Want was an uncomplicated emotion, easily felt, easily satiated. Patrick assured himself that all it would take to get Carly out of his mind was to get her into his bed. Then, once his curiosity and desire were satisfied, he could get on with his life.

In no mood to greet visitors, he didn't get up for the doorbell, waiting instead for the unwelcome intruder to give up and go away. But whoever it was appeared to have no intention of leaving, and finally, muttering a soft oath, Patrick made his way to the door.

"What are you doing here?" he asked, staring down at Carly standing on his top step.

"May I come in?" she asked calmly, looking past him into the darkened hallway. She couldn't see any signs of another woman. But perhaps that was why the house was so dark.

"Of course. Let me take your coat."

"Thank you." She slipped out of the scarlet wool cape and handed it to him. "I hope I wasn't interrupting anything."

"Nothing important." Patrick was unwilling to let her know he'd been sitting alone in the dark, sulking.

"Good." She walked past him, into the den. "Are you conserving energy?" she asked conversationally. "It's awfully dark in here, Patrick."

"I like it that way. What are you doing here, Carly?"

She had been asking herself that same question all the way there. Her first impulse had been to ask him about Julia, straight out. Fortunately, by the time she had pulled up in front of Patrick's Georgetown house, she had decided discretion was the better part of valor. At least for now. After all, hadn't she accused Patrick of rushing their relationship? Although patience was not one of Carly's strong suits, she forced herself to remain noncommittal.

"I wanted some company," she answered. "Since you seem to be working around the clock, I took a chance on finding you still up."

"What's the matter with Alex?"

Carly studied Patrick carefully, alerted by his gritty tone. It was the same one he'd used when they had discussed the concert this morning. Was it possible he was actually jealous? She decided she rather liked that idea.

"Nothing. Alex is always delightful company. I was just driving home when I realized that I wasn't at all sleepy." She smiled. "I think I'm still a little high from Mangione."

Patrick thought he had detected an air of nervousness about Carly when she had first arrived. While he didn't think she was a liar, he also didn't believe she was telling him the entire story. Why was she here?

"I take it he put on a good show," he said, giving up on figuring out anything about Carly for the moment. She was as elusive as a butterfly; just when he thought he had begun to figure her out, she'd go flitting off into some new direction.

She sighed happily. "Divine." She looked past him toward the billiard table. "Do you play?"

"Some. How about you?"

"My grandfather tried to teach me, but I had an unfortunate tendency to sink the cue ball."

While he could think of several more appealing ways to pass the time with Carly, Patrick accepted the invitation in her tone. Anything to keep her here.

"Feel up to a game?"

"It depends on how much we're betting. How do I know that you aren't a hustler?"

He laughed at that. "Name your stakes."

"Dinner. Loser pays."

"You're on," Patrick agreed, turning on a light. He took a pair of cue sticks down from the rack on the wall, giving Carly her choice. "What do you want to play?" he asked as he placed the balls into the triangular rack, nudging them tight.

Carly frowned, eyeing the table. "I'm not certain I remember the logistics."

Patrick dismissed her concerns. "That's okay—you'll catch on in no time. How about eight ball? Since you're company, I'll let you break."

"That's very nice of you, Patrick." She scanned the balls thoughtfully. "Eight ball—isn't that stripes and solids?"

"That's it."

"I suppose I can handle that," she mused aloud as she took a worn cube of blue chalk and rubbed it slowly against the tip of her cue. "Do you happen to have any talc?"

A niggling suspicion probed at his mind, but Patrick immediately dismissed it. "Over there." He nodded toward the rack, watching with interest as Carly applied a layer of the talc along the ridge of her thumb and index finger.

"That's better," she murmured. She set the cue ball at the head of the table, positioning the cue between her fingers. A swift, fluid stroke of the stick scattered the pack of balls. Seconds later the three ball fell into the corner pocket.

"That means I have the solids, right?" she asked, looking at him over her shoulder. "And you have stripes."

"I see it's coming back to you," Patrick answered dryly.

Carly tossed him an innocent smile. "A bit."

Her eyes narrowed as she scrutinized the table, studying the arrangement. As Patrick watched, she executed a bank shot that put the six ball into the side pocket. She sank the four ball next, then moved around the table, studying a corner to corner shot. The two ball disappeared.

"Nice shot," Patrick offered.

"Thank you," Carly responded absently. She frowned slightly, then took the bridge from the wall and set it on the table, placing her cue on top of it. "I hear your father is staging a filibuster," she said as she shot. The seven ball dropped from sight.

"He enjoys an opportunity to hold center stage. I don't know what he's going to do when he retires."

A short stroke, cutting the cue ball low for a backspin, sank the five. "So it's true? He really isn't going to run for reelection?"

"That's what he says. Although I'll believe it when I see it. . . . I have the feeling I've been hustled."

"Nonsense," Carly replied serenely.

Her teeth chewed at her lower lip as she moved around the table. Patrick backed away, giving her room. The enticing scent of white roses drifted upward from her skin, momentarily clouding his mind. As she bent over, he leaned on his cue, thoroughly enjoying the view.

Carly set her hand onto the bright green felt and laid the cue across it. She smiled, pleased, as the ball skidded into the side pocket.

"Eight ball in the corner pocket," she stated, eyeing the position of the final ball. Patrick was not at all surprised when it fell, exactly as predicted.

She stood up, her eyes sparkling. "Where are you taking me for dinner, Patrick?"

Patrick laughed, feeling unreasonably lighthearted. "Anywhere the lady likes," he said. "And since I'm a gentleman, I won't point out that pool hustling is against the law."

Carly arched a blond eyebrow. "Honestly, Patrick, I don't know what you're talking about." Her grin broke free. "Want to try again? Double or nothing? You can break," she offered expansively.

They played two more games, Patrick sweeping the table to win the second. The final game was more evenly contested, but Patrick was finding it more and more difficult to concentrate. The red knit hugged her slender curves in a way that was definitely disconcerting and the soft scent of her perfume continued to tease at his mind. He was setting up a bank shot when she came to stand beside him, watching silently. The enticing warmth of her body caused a white-hot flame to spark within him.

He shot. They both watched as the ball bounced off a cushion, into the middle of the table.

"I guess it's my shot," Carly said, chalking her cue.

Patrick reached out, stopping her progress as she tried to move around the table. His fingers curved around her waist.

"Your grandfather taught you well."

His touch was causing her heart to beat faster. Carly wondered if he could feel the intensity of her pulse under his fingertips.

"I told you we spent a lot of time in Elks' lodges. They all have pool tables."

His gaze was focused on her lips. "Did he teach you to cheat, as well?"

"Cheat?" she asked haltingly, shaken by the lambent flame in his eyes. "I haven't cheated."

His fingers tightened. "Of course you have. You cheat every time you walk by me, smelling like a soft summer meadow. You cheat by wearing a dress designed to inspire masculine fantasies." His cue dropped to the floor unheeded and his free hand stroked her hair. The smooth blond strands carried the lingering scent of citrus. "I have a suggestion."

Carly took a deep breath. "A suggestion?"

He plucked the cue stick from her nerveless fingers, tossing it uncaringly atop the table. "Let's find some other game to play. Something a bit more challenging." His hand tunneled under her hair to cup the back of her neck.

Carly forced herself to meet his gaze, finding passion in his eyes. But there was pain there, as well. A pain she was beginning to understand. She reminded herself that Patrick was not yet prepared to share his secrets with her. What was the point in succumbing to sexual desire when he steadfastly refused to offer any real intimacy of spirit?

"I believe you've just raised the stakes," she managed to state with feigned calm, even as she twisted her fingers together nervously behind her back.

Patrick drew her against his chest. "You know I want you, Carly."

She nodded slowly.

His broad hands stroked her back, urging her to give in. "If you didn't want the night to end like this, why did you come here in the first place?"

There was a long moment of silence before Carly answered. "I wanted to get to know you better," she said finally. When he retrieved her hands to lift them around his neck Carly found herself unable to resist.

"I can think of a lot better ways to accomplish that than by playing pool." His deep voice tolled in her ear as his teeth nibbled lightly, enticingly, at the tender skin of her lobe.

"You make it sound so simple," Carly protested softly.

His lips trailed down her throat, warming her skin as he unsettled her mind. "It is." He brushed a gentle kiss against her trembling lips. "Come into the bedroom with me, Carly. Let me love you."

"Patrick." Struggling with the dual desires of both mind and body, Carly leaned against him, even as she continued to protest.

Patrick pressed her back against the table, his need evident as his body surged against hers. "Don't fight the inevitable," he murmured. "You're a woman who thrives on acting on your feelings, Carly. Don't turn analytical on me now."

That was just the point, she could have argued. Despite her admittedly strong desire for Patrick, she had other feelings every bit as intense that were warning her against involvement with a man who possessed so many dark secrets. Perhaps it was wishing for the moon, but Carly found herself wanting more from Patrick than a few hours of sexual bliss. What she wanted was the one thing she was afraid he'd never be prepared to give. His love.

Patrick traced Carly's trembling lips gently with his thumb. She remained silent, closing her eyes to his enticing touch as his fingers caressed the slender planes of her face. Who could have imagined that such a strong, unyielding man could be so tender?

Patrick knew that he was not alone in his desire. So why did Carly continue to set up these roadblocks? "Do you still believe I'm going to steal Capitol away from you?" he asked, seeking the key.

Carly's eyes flew open. "Of course not."

His knuckles brushed sparks along her cheekbone. "Then you do trust me?"

The wild beat of her heart thundered in her ears. "Sometimes," she whispered on a fractured sigh.

His fingers played in her hair, tangling in the strands that reminded him of wild honey. "But not all the time."

Her hands seemed to have a mind of their own as her palms moved across the rigid line of his shoulders, reveling in the solid flesh shaping the soft chambray shirt.

"Not all the time," she agreed raggedly, torn by the storm Patrick was creating within her.

As raw hunger clamored for release, Patrick reminded himself that he had been working around the clock the past month, familiarizing himself with Capitol Airline's financial situation. Two months ago he had been immersed in negotiations for that copper company, and before that he had successfully mediated a strike threat at a southern carpet mill.

He had gone a very long time without a woman; any man who had led a celibate existence for so long would be responding to Carly Ashton. Just as he would be reacting precisely the same way to any other attractive, desirable female. That was all it was—sexual need. That was all he would allow it to be.

Even as he tried to convince himself of that fact, Patrick experienced misgivings. There was something both alluring and dangerous about Carly. Some inner force that had him experiencing emotions he thought he had successfully buried five years ago.

He forced his mind back to his immediate goal of getting Carly into his bed. "Is this one of those times that you don't trust me?"

Afraid to speak, Carly nodded.

He gazed at her steadily, watching apprehension and desire war in her deep violet-blue eyes. Unable to resist the appeal of her lips, he lowered his head, covering her mouth with his. He fought against the urge to crush her against him, keeping the kiss soft, his lips nibbling with a featherlike pressure.

Carly closed her eyes, succumbing to the surprising gentleness of the kiss. She had been prepared for a devastating show of hungry passion; that she could have resisted. But this unexpected tenderness caused a blissful cloud of lassitude to settle over her. She relaxed, leaning against him, her fingers linked behind his neck.

As Carly's sigh of contentment drifted into his mouth, Patrick realized he had regained the upper hand. The power was his; he could use it as he wished. Oddly enough, at this moment, he only wanted to bring her pleasure.

"You are delectable," he murmured, whispering kisses over her face, lingering for a moment on her closed eyelids before moving on to her temple. Her pulse leaped at the touch of his lips, and she moaned softly.

Patrick trailed his lips down her neck. "Delightful."

When his deft fingers slid the zipper at the back of her dress down a few inches, Carly whispered a protest. But Patrick's mouth returned to hers, swallowing the words. He pushed the scarlet material aside, giving him access to her collarbone, and Carly felt herself tumbling headfirst into disaster as his tongue skimmed along her skin.

"Mmm, you are also delicious," he professed, his hand gliding down her body to settle possessively over her heart. He could feel her blood beating under his palm like the frantic fluttering of a wild bird's wings.

"That's enough," she protested weakly, struggling to maintain some sense of sanity. Her hands pressed against his shoulders.

Patrick's arms tightened around her, holding her to him when she would have moved away. "There's where you're wrong, sweetheart," he corrected. His mouth turned greedy, claiming dominance as he deepened the kiss, urging her further into submission.

Every cell in her body was crying out for release, and it took more self-control than Carly had known she possessed to resist Patrick's expert seduction.

His lips grazed her cheek as she twisted her head, pulling far enough away to look up at him. "It's time for me to go home," she insisted. Her breathing was ragged, her words fractured, but Patrick had no trouble understanding her message. Her body had stiffened resolutely in his arms.

He sighed heavily as he released her. "Whatever you say, sweetheart, although I'll be damned if I can figure out why you insist on postponing the inevitable."

Carly hated it when he behaved so remotely, treating what was happening between them as nothing more than an impersonal sexual interlude. She let out a hiss of breath.

"Perhaps it's because I don't consider an affair inevitable."

His answering oath was short and surprisingly savage. "I want you; you want me; we're both adults. So what's the problem?" he inquired heatedly.

At the unexpected flare of temper blazing in his eyes, Carly took an automatic step backward, finding her retreat blocked by the pool table.

"I don't want you," she tossed back.

Her words created a burst of anger that surprised Patrick with its intensity. His life had been devoid of strong emotion these past years; he had made certain of that. He had almost forgotten that like all the members of the Ryan clan, he possessed a fierce Irish temper.

"Liar."

His fiery eyes burned into her and for the first time since meeting Patrick, she could envision him as Senator Mike Ryan's son. Patrick's father's incendiary temperament was as well known as his liberal political views. Eyeing Patrick warily, Carly decided it must run in their blood.

"All right," she admitted hastily, when it appeared he was going to pull her into his arms to disprove her words. "I may be attracted to you. But I don't want anything you have to offer."

She half expected an eruption that would make Mount St. Helen's appear docile, but Patrick surprised Carly by laughing, a harsh, bitter sound.

"Join the club, sweetheart." He leaned toward Carly, his glowering face a few inches from hers. "What makes you think you're what I want? Ever since I arrived in Washington, you've disrupted my work, caused me too many sleepless nights and distracted me from my goal of rescuing your blasted airline.

"The one thing I insist on from my women is that they don't make demands. And they damn well don't interfere with my work! Or my mind!"

Carly brushed by him, her head erect, her spine stiff. "Well, since I have no intention of being one of your women, we shouldn't have any more problems," she snapped. "Go get one of those empty-headed paragons," Carly suggested acidly. "Some safe, undemanding Barbie Doll who doesn't make you doubt your feelings. Just leave me the hell alone." She marched from the room.

Fury rose within Patrick as he heard the front door slam. Picking up the pool cue from the floor, he flung it onto the green felt. Balls scattered in all directions on the table, disappearing from view.

AS SHE GOT DRESSED the next morning, Carly instructed herself not to think about last night's debacle. The thing to do was to put Patrick Ryan completely from her mind and begin acting like a rational adult. She continued her little pep talk as she drove to work in a cold, drizzling winter rain. Under normal conditions, Carly was not one of those people who found rain depressing, but this morning the weather seemed to be echoing her own dreary mood. Her mind continually drifted back to the highly unsatisfactory end to what had started out to be a delightful evening.

Carly could not remember the last time she had met anyone who could aggravate her the way Patrick Ryan was continually doing. She had been telling him the truth when she suggested he brought out the worst in her. Growing up with her grandfather and his odd assortment of cronies had taught her to be generous in her response to others. Even as a child, Carly had never resented her mother's behavior in abandoning her. She had accepted the fact that Bettina Ashton was simply not mother material. Surely it was better to have grown up with someone who welcomed her presence in his life, rather than to have been seen as a burden.

Carly tried to make concessions for people's flaws, seeking instead positive attributes that would enable her to get along with almost anyone. So why was it so difficult to behave the same way with Patrick? Her feelings had been swinging back and forth like an out of control pendulum ever since their first meeting.

She had forgotten to buy new windshield wipers and the irritating squeal of torn rubber and metal on glass served to distract her from her depressing thoughts. As the icy streaks slid unhampered down her windshield, Carly shook her head, refusing to wallow in her atypical melancholy.

This had to stop! Although it wouldn't be easy, considering the fact that they were forced to work together, Carly was a firm believer in the power of positive thinking. A person could do anything if she just put her mind to it, she assured herself as she entered Capitol's offices.

"Mr. Ryan will be out of the office most of the morning," Marge offered as Carly cast a tentative glance toward the closed door of the executive office. "He's meeting with some of the creditors."

"I wish him luck," Carly mumbled as she deposited her umbrella into the brass holder and hung her plum slicker on the matching rack.

Darn the man anyway! It was difficult to be furious with him when he was out working to save her career. Reminding herself that his actions were not in the least bit altruistic—after all, he was earning a hefty fee—she entered her own office, determined to lose herself in work.

Her firm intentions disintegrated like a sand castle at high tide when she saw the vase of sunshine-yellow flowers. Daffodils. Where on earth did one find daffodils in February?

Marge was standing in the doorway. "They were here when I arrived this morning," she stated. "Aren't they gorgeous?"

"Lovely," Carly admitted reluctantly, plucking the card from the dark green foliage. "They reminded me of you," she read.

"Damn," she muttered under her breath.

Marge arched a tawny brow. "I can think of more appropriate responses."

Carly sank into the chair behind her desk, regarding the bright flowers as if they were a poisonous snake poised to strike. "He's driving me up the wall."

"I'd be in seventh heaven if that man ever sent me flowers," Marge offered helpfully.

Carly looked at her curiously. "How do you know they're from Patrick?"

Marge laughed. "How many other men do you know who could locate daffodils in the middle of the night? In winter?"

Carly sighed. "Just one," she admitted. "But if he believes these change anything, he'd better think again. From now on, it's strictly business where Patrick Ryan and I are concerned."

Marge's green eyes sparkled with amusement. "This sounds like a case of the irresistible force running headlong into the immovable object. If I were a betting woman, I'd have to put my money on Mr. Ryan. But good luck, anyway," she advised, returning to her own desk.

More than once that morning, Carly reached toward the vase, determined to dump the daffodils into the wastebasket. Each time she stopped, unable to do so. She told herself it was only because they added such a cheery note to the dismal gray day.

She heard Patrick return after lunch; his tone, when he greeted Marge expansively, revealed that his meetings had gone well. Carly only hoped the one with the pilots scheduled for next week would turn out as well. She did her best to avoid him, but when Marge buzzed her, telling her Patrick wanted to see her, Carly knew the moment had come to put her resolutions to the test.

"How did everything go?" she asked casually as she entered his office. She took a chair opposite him.

Patrick smiled. "Better than I had expected. Let's hope I'm on a roll."

"Are you really expecting that much trouble from the pilots?"

He shrugged. "It won't be a piece of cake. I'd like you to sit in on that meeting next Tuesday, if you're not too busy."

"Of course I will," Carly agreed immediately. "Although I don't know what I can do."

His gaze warmed as his eyes held hers. "Let's just say I could use someone in my corner."

Carly felt her resolve melting. It was so difficult to remain angry with him when he looked at her that way. "Thank you for the flowers," she said softly.

"Consider it a peace offering," Patrick suggested. He smiled encouragingly. "I was out of line last night, Carly. I'm sorry."

For a long, silent moment, Carly could only stare at him. "Is the great Patrick Ryan actually admitting he was wrong?" she inquired finally. "Perhaps I should have Marge call the *Post*. They'll want to run this amazing bit of news on the front page."

"With banner headlines," he added amiably.

Carly brushed at a nonexistent piece of lint on her electric-blue wool skirt. "Sorry isn't a word you toss around lightly, Patrick."

It was impossible to miss the unspoken question in her tone. "You're right," Patrick stated. "I save it for the important things. Important people."

She slowly lifted her head. "Am I one of those people?"

He answered her question with one of his own. "What do you think?"

Carly sighed. "Quite honestly, Patrick, I don't know what to think right now."

They exchanged a long, searching gaze. For a moment, Patrick looked inclined to say something, but changed his mind, turning the subject instead to the lease agreement for the new planes.

Carly struggled to keep her mind on the pages of legalese, but as she watched his finger move down the paper, emphasizing various clauses, she couldn't help wondering how those hands would feel on her body. He'd be strong, she determined. But gentle. Any man who gave a woman daffodils on a rainy February morning would know how to be tender.

When she heard him repeating her name, Carly realized she had not been paying attention. Expelling a short breath that ruffled her bangs, she forced her attention back to the lease agreement.

"Carry on, Patrick," she encouraged brightly. "I'm fascinated."

Patrick studied her curiously for a moment. Then, shrugging his shoulders, he continued reading.

9

THE FOLLOWING TUESDAY, Patrick kept his promise and offered Marge a promotion. The efficient young woman readily agreed to delay taking on her new duties until after Capitol's current crisis had passed. Admittedly relieved, Carly saw no reason to postpone a celebratory lunch.

The proximity of the Maison Blanche, next door to the White House, made it a favorite of statesmen and celebrities. As one might expect, given the clientele, the tables were widely spaced for privacy, the waiters appropriately discreet.

"Mr. McIntyre sounded a lot better when I talked with him today," Marge said after they had ordered.

"He does, doesn't he?" Carly agreed with a smile. "You know, I really miss him."

"He's a nice man. Not as sexy as Mr. Ryan, but nice." She grinned. "Even if he has been stonewalling my promotion."

Carly stared at Marge for a moment, then she laughed. "I should have known nothing at Capitol ever gets by you."

Marge ran a perfectly manicured fingernail around the rim of her wineglass. "I do my best to keep abreast of things. Including the fact that you and our fearless leader are an item."

Carly took a sip of her chilled white wine. "I don't know what you're talking about."

"Don't you?" Marge's lips curved into a smile. "Come on, Carly, anyone can see that you two have a lot more going than union negotiations and bankruptcy proceedings. Patrick's head snaps up every time you walk by his office door. And you spend half your time staring off into space, like some love-struck teenager."

Before Carly could answer, they were interrupted by the waiter, delivering their order. Both women fell silent as he placed the crisp salads in front of them, along with a basket of fresh, warm rolls. After refilling their water glasses, he retreated.

Carly picked up her fork and took a bite of spinach greens. "Delicious."

"You're stalling," Marge pointed out accurately.

"And you're pushing," Carly retorted. Realizing that she had raised her voice, she glanced quickly around the room, seeming assured that the other diners were engrossed in their own conversations.

"I'm sorry," Carly apologized. "It's just that my relationship with Patrick is not one of my favorite topics of conversation. Have some bread," she suggested, pushing the basket toward Marge, who ignored it.

"Got it rough, huh, kiddo?" Marge inquired solicitously.

Carly speared an artichoke heart. "Do you believe in love at first sight?"

"I'm a firm believer in love any way a woman can get it." Her laughing green eyes sobered. "You're serious, aren't you?"

Carly tapped a fingernail thoughtfully against the stem of her wineglass. "I've been trying to figure out when, exactly, I fell in love with him," she admitted. "But it's as if I can't remember a time I didn't love him." She shook her head. "It just doesn't make any sense."

"Love isn't supposed to," Marge pointed out. "Lord knows, I've been through it enough times to be an expert."

"How can you stand it?" Carly asked, distress evident in her tone. "I thought love was supposed to make you feel wonderful, like you were walking on air." She frowned down at the tablecloth. "I've been feeling more and more as if I've been run over by a train." Blue eyes lifted, laced with obvious distress.

"What does Patrick have to say about all this?"

Carly's gaze drifted around the restaurant. "We haven't discussed it," she said finally.

Marge waited until Carly's eyes returned to hers. "I can't believe that. Both of you are the type of people who speak their minds, straight out."

"The subject hasn't come up," Carly repeated firmly.

Marge's puzzled frown faded, replaced by a slow, understanding smile as comprehension dawned. "I get it. Patrick's talking sex, so you're not talking at all."

"Something like that," Carly mumbled.

Marge laughed lightly. "Carly, a man like Patrick Ryan doesn't fall all over himself the way he's been doing, just to win a bed partner. He doesn't have to. You know as well as I do that this town is filled with women who'd tumble into the sack at a crook of his little finger."

"Would you?"

"Probably," Marge returned mildly. "If the man showed one inkling of interest. But the fact is, Carly, the only woman he wants is you. And if I were you, I wouldn't waste my time waiting for a declaration of undying love. Take what you can get—that's always been my motto."

"And if I want more?"

Marge put her napkin onto the table. "Believe me, kiddo, the heart is the most amazing organ in the body. It can be broken over and over again and just when you think that this time you're a goner, some handsome hunk strolls into your life and you wake up in the morning realizing you've just undergone another miracle cure."

As she paid the check, Carly wished that she could maintain Marge's casual outlook on life. But they were different individuals, with different desires, different needs. Carly froze, momentarily focusing on that one word. *Need*. It was so much more insidious than want; the entire idea connoted a weakness that she disliked discovering in herself. As she drove back to the office for the afternoon meeting with the representatives from the pilots' union, Carly forced the discomforting thought from her mind.

THE MEETING DID NOT GO WELL. Highly skilled and well paid, the pilots obviously resented the proposed cutbacks Patrick insisted were necessary to keep Capitol flying. Carly watched with admiration as Patrick used finesse, refraining from steamrollering over the objections in an attempt to gain the upper hand.

"I still think we're getting a raw deal," Warren Baker, the most senior of the pilots complained. He had served as spokesman for the group during most of the meeting. "You're asking us to give away a helluva lot more than the machinists or the flight attendants."

"I believe the figures will disprove that," Patrick stated calmly.

Baker ran a hand across the steel-gray crew cut he'd worn for the past twenty years. "Why in the hell should we trust your figures? Everyone knows how McIntyre lives. He's got a lot of nerve, asking us to cut back while he basks in the lap of luxury." The other two pilots nodded in agreement.

"You're not dealing with McIntyre," Patrick pointed out. "You're dealing with me."

Baker made a gesture of dismissal. "So? Management has maintained a fighter-pilot mentality around this place for the past two years. What makes you any different?"

At his challenging tone, Carly expected a flare of anger from Patrick. But he remained calm, outwardly unmoved by the older man's accusation.

"Since we're offering you representation on the board, you'll gain a say in corporate policy," Patrick reminded the man. "In addition, if you honestly don't trust our figures, you're invited to bring in your own auditing firm. Just remember that we are facing a deadline. We don't have all the time in the world."

"I still think it's a dumb idea," Baker grumbled. "We're pilots, not desk jockeys. I've got a good idea how much clout we'd gain on the board. We'd probably be relegated to all the important, earthshattering decisions like wallpaper and furniture choices. Why should we give a damn what color you paint your fancy executive offices?"

Carly couldn't remain silent any longer. "Warren, there are a lot of important issues that management and labor can work together on. As allies, not enemies. Things far more important than wallpaper."

Her gaze swept the office a moment before returning to the three pilots. "Besides, management didn't have any more say in the decorating of these offices than labor." She smiled. "Bill hired a very bossy architect, who in turn hired an absolute dragon of a decorator. This, gentlemen," she professed, gesturing around the room, "was a take it or leave it proposition."

"Which is a far cry from what we're offering you," Patrick stated. "We're offering a stake in your own futures."

"We already came up with a plan to secure our futures," Baker returned instantly. "And McIntyre threw it out the window."

Patrick leaned back in his chair, appearing relaxed, though Carly suspected otherwise. If there was one demand Capitol could never agree to, it was the union's proposal for a set percentage of gross revenue.

"Come on, Baker," Patrick said with a patient smile, "you know there isn't a company anywhere in the country who'd go along with that plan. It's a sure path to destruction."

The senior pilot bristled. "That's what management says. We say differently."

Patrick exchanged a long look with Carly. Stifling a sigh, he leaned forward, his arms braced on the desktop. "In the first place, you're asking for ten and a half cents of every dollar of Capitol's revenue. You're an intelligent man, Baker. You can't honestly be recommending a compensation program that focuses solely on gross revenue and ignores expenses." Patrick shook his head, rejecting the idea entirely. "We have to spend money to make money; we can't tie up our cash flow like that. Besides, it's unfair to the workers in the other unions and the noncontract people."

"Let them worry about themselves," Matt Armstrong, one of the other pilots, put in. "We've got families to feed. We need to look out for our futures."

"If Capitol folds because of selfish and naive demands, you won't have any futures," Patrick countered abruptly. Regretting his momentary loss of control, he took a deep breath and tried again.

"Look, I think we've gone about as far as we can today. Take this to your board, discuss it with your rank and file and get back to us, all right?"

Baker rose first, the other two men following his lead. "We'll take it back, but I sure as hell wouldn't hold your breath, Ryan."

Patrick came to his feet, holding out his hand. "It's a whole new ball game out there, Baker. Management and labor are both facing a crisis. The only way we're going to be able to survive is drop the old antagonistic attitudes and create a new system."

The pilot shook his head, ignoring Patrick's outstretched hand. "You may be smoother than the union busters they used to bring in, Ryan. But you're still cut from the same cloth; they're just packaging it in a prettier manner these days."

Once the three men had filed from the office, Patrick swept his hand furiously across the desk, scattering papers and ledger sheets all over the floor.

"Damn!" he ground out, shoving his hands into his back pockets as he glared out the window.

Understanding his frustration with the way the meeting had gone, Carly remained silent, giving him time to control his temper. She knelt down, gathering up the pieces of what she knew to be a brilliant proposal.

"You were right," she said finally.

Patrick didn't turn away from the window. "About what?"

"That the pilots would prove difficult." She sighed, sinking into the chair Warren Baker had abandoned. "I never would have guessed it."

"It's Baker who's the joker in the deck," Patrick muttered. "He's grabbing for power with both hands and the idiot doesn't realize he's dragging everyone down with him."

When Patrick finally turned around, his face wore a grim smile. "Remind me never to fly with that guy. I think he'd ditch the plane on general principles."

"He has an excellent flying record," Carly felt obliged to point out.

Patrick returned to his chair, dragging his hand wearily over his face. Carly wished she could do something to lighten the mood in the room.

"Would you get me Baker's personnel file?" he requested suddenly.

Carly picked up the telephone receiver, speaking for a few moments to the clerk in personnel. Then she reached over, turning on the compact desk computer.

"It's coming up on the screen now."

Shoving the dark-rimmed reading glasses onto his face, Patrick leaned toward the computer. "Here it is," he said triumphantly a moment later. "At least now we know where Baker is coming from."

"Arizona?" Carly asked blankly, looking over his shoulder.

"That's a copper town," Patrick explained, tapping the screen with his pen where Warren Baker's place of birth was listed. "I'll bet you next month's revenue that his father was a copper miner."

"A union copper miner," she echoed, a light beginning to flicker in the back of her mind.

Patrick nodded. "Now all we have to do is convince Baker that we're not robber barons," he said, leaning back in his chair.

"And you can do that, can't you?"

Patrick snapped his fingers. "Piece of cake," he agreed with slightly more confidence than he was feeling at the moment. But he had never allowed a failure in his negotiations, and he wasn't about to begin now.

Patrick's enthusiasm was contagious, and Carly found herself returning his smile. The mood in the room changed, becoming suddenly charged with an intimacy that belied the unsatisfactory meeting they had just concluded.

Patrick's eyes darkened as they settled on her upturned lips. "Carly..."

She shook her head, denying him the opportunity to discuss anything personal. "Not now," she protested quietly.

"When? We have to talk about it."

She expelled a slight sigh. He was right of course. "I don't know. Perhaps after all this is over."

He waved away her suggestion with his hand. "I don't want to wait that long."

"Do you always get everything you want?" she asked softly.

"Always." There was a challenge in his tone. Then, not wanting to press his luck, Patrick took a deep breath and began again. "What would you say to discussing it over dinner?"

"Dinner?"

"I owe you one, remember?"

That silly bet. Carly had forgotten all about it. "That's not necessary. Besides, Patrick, you were right. I did hustle you. Just a little."

His smile didn't quite reach his eyes. "I'm not one to welsh on a bet, Carly. You and I are having dinner together. Tonight."

"I have a date," she ad-libbed the lie.

Patrick appeared to ignore her as he turned his attention back to the stack of papers on his desk. Just when Carly thought she had gotten off scot-free, he proved her wrong.

"Break it," he instructed. When she opened her mouth to protest, he lifted his coaxing gaze to her blistering one. "Please?"

Carly crossed her arms over her chest. "Why should I do that?" she inquired archly.

"Because we have to work together, Carly. And we're not going to be able to pull this off if we keep getting distracted by our personal feelings." He held her challenging gaze with the sheer strength of his will. "If you're not worried about your own career," he suggested, "you could at least think about your absent partner."

"Holding Bill's future over my head is a dirty trick," she protested heatedly.

Patrick appeared unperturbed by her renewed spark of anger. "I thought we had already determined that I cheat whenever necessary," he responded conversationally.

He had boxed her into a neat little corner and even as Carly was irritated by his methods, she had to give him credit for his ability to control things to his own liking. She was beginning to understand Alex's accusation that Patrick always played by his own rules.

"All right," she said. "But I'm only agreeing to this for Bill's sake."

"Whatever you say," he responded amiably, the flash of victory in his eyes letting Carly know that he didn't believe her for a moment. "Now, shall we get back to business?"

"I think that's a good idea."

Carly returned to her own office, spending the remainder of the afternoon wading through a mountain of paperwork. Her correspondence was varied and often amusing as she answered letters ranging from an elderly Kansas City woman actually requesting the recipe for a meat loaf served on her flight to Springfield, to an invitation to speak at the Baltimore Business and Professional Women's annual banquet.

It was after six o'clock when she reentered Patrick's office. "How good a mood are you in?" she asked.

Patrick glanced up from his paperwork. "That sounds suspiciously like a trick question."

"I've got Clayton from the machinists on line one. He says they have problems with the offer."

Expelling a short, rude oath, Patrick put down his pencil and picked up the receiver. "Clayton," he greeted the union representative expansively, "what can I do for you this evening?"

Carly watched a frown deepen Patrick's brow. "I explained all that. Tell them it's not a simple profit sharing plan. It's an employee stock option buyout plan."

He took off his glasses, rubbing tiredly at the red mark darkening the bridge of his nose. "That's right, they'll be part owners.... That's right. All together the unions will end up with twenty-five percent of the company."

He glanced up at Carly, who was watching him anxiously. "Yes, it is unusual," he agreed, returning his attention to the man on the other end of the line. "Yes, I thought that might prove an incentive.... Thanks, I plan to. You have a good evening, too."

Patrick hung up the phone and drew a slow, deep breath. When he lifted his head, his bright eyes belied the weariness Carly knew he must be experiencing.

"Bingo," he said with a broad, victorious grin. "Clayton's going to poll his members tonight. But he thinks they'll go for it."

How strange that he could create such havoc in her body with a mere smile. At this moment, Carly knew that she would probably agree to anything Patrick was willing to offer.

"I was wrong about you," she said suddenly.

A wary look appeared in Patrick's eyes. "Wrong about me?"

Perching on the edge of the desk, she reached out to trace his grimly set mouth with her fingernail. "About you," she agreed softly. "You are my white knight, after all."

Experiencing a cooling rush of relief, Patrick caught her hand in his. His crystal-blue eyes deepened to gleaming sapphire and as his free hand stroked her nylon-clad calf, Carly felt her bones melt.

"Ready to call it a day?" he asked.

Afraid to trust her voice, Carly nodded.

"You have a choice," he offered. "We can go out to some crowded, noisy restaurant, or we can settle for Chinese at my place."

Throwing caution to the wind, Carly answered without a moment's hesitation. "That sounds great, Patrick. I love Chinese food."

10

BY THE TIME THEY'D PICKED UP their dinner and returned to Patrick's house, the sensual mood had given way to one of comfortable companionship. Sometime later, Patrick leaned back on his elbows, his legs stretched out, as he watched Carly with unabashed pleasure. She was sitting cross-legged on the floor in front of his fireplace, surrounded by white cardboard cartons. Her enthusiasm for the varied fare equaled that of a woman sifting through the jewelry trays at Cartiers.

"I absolutely adore these ribs," she said as she licked the sweet-and-sour sauce from her fingers. "Are you certain you don't want this last one?"

"It's all yours."

"Thank you, Patrick. That's very generous of you."

"Think nothing of it," he drawled, leaning forward to re-fill their teacups. "May I ask a personal question?"

"I suppose so," she agreed absently, plunging her chopsticks into a carton of butterfly fried shrimp.

"How can you eat like a long haul trucker and stay so slim?"

"I've got good metabolism," Carly answered when she had finished chewing. "Plus, I burn a lot of calories dancing."

Patrick eyed her over the rim of his cup. "Speaking of that, when are you going to grant me a command performance?"

"That's right," Carly remembered, plucking a crisp wonton from yet another carton, "you like tap-dancing."

When she reached for a second, Patrick took the chopsticks from her, retrieving the deep-fried noodle himself. He held it out to her.

"Correction. I like tap dancers."

The rising flame in Patrick's blue eyes assured Carly that at the moment he was referring to one recreational tap dancer in particular.

"Patrick," she murmured, "you're making me extremely nervous."

"Good. Because I've been a basket case for the past week and a half.... Aren't you hungry?"

"I think I've had enough," she demurred. Her voice was thin, devoid of its usual throaty timbre, and Carly wondered whether fear or excitement had her suddenly frozen to the spot.

Patrick's lips curved enticingly. "Come on, Carly," he coaxed, his voice flowing over her like melted honey, "take a bite. I think I like the idea of you eating out of my hand."

"Now that I can believe. Really, Patrick, I couldn't eat another bite."

"You're not going to pass up dessert?"

Carly groaned. "I hope it isn't anything too rich. I knew I'd regret eating all that lobster Cantonese."

Patrick held out a small white paper bag. "You can't have an authentic Chinese dinner without fortune cookies, Carly. Come on," he encouraged with a winning smile, "I'll even give you first choice."

Carly had never been able to resist fortune cookies. It wasn't that she believed in them, of course. But there *had* been those odd occasions when they had come uncannily close to predicting upcoming events. She hesitated, the decision suddenly irrationally important. Finally, closing her eyes, she plunged her hand into the bag, quickly retrieving a crisp cookie. She cracked it open and extracted the slender strip of paper.

"What does it say?" Patrick asked.

It doesn't mean anything, Carly assured herself as she read the message. *They print these up by the thousands. Anyone could have gotten it.* It was simply a coincidence.

"Carly?"

"You haven't opened yours," she hedged.

Patrick's eyes were thoughtful as they scanned her face, searching for secrets. Then he shrugged and broke open the remaining cookie. "'He who hesitates is not only lost, but miles from the next exit.'" He arched a dark brow. "This is an ancient Chinese saying?"

"I suppose even fortune cookies have to keep up with the times," Carly offered.

Patrick crumpled the paper, tossing it back into the bag. "I suppose so. But it sure as hell isn't Confucius. What does yours say?"

"It's silly."

"Now you've got me curious." He reached out and plucked the paper from her fingers. "'The dictates of the heart are the voice of fate,'" he read aloud. He lifted his head and gave her a slow, dangerous smile. "Interesting."

"Really, Patrick," Carly protested, rising to her feet, "it's just a stupid fortune cookie. They all sound the same."

A log broke on the fire, sending forth a spray of crackling sparks. Both ignored it.

Patrick felt a burst of temper surging through him. Not tonight, he warned himself. The one thing he didn't want to do was drive Carly away again. Needing time to control his emotions, he refrained from answering immediately. Instead, he gathered up the cartons and took them into the kitchen. Pressing his palms against the counter, he drew in several deep, calming breaths. When he returned, his eyes held a devilish gleam.

"Are you actually going to ignore the advice of some ancient Chinese philosopher?"

"I don't even think that's Chinese," Carly argued.

"Probably not," Patrick agreed readily. "But it makes a great deal of sense." He crossed the span of Oriental carpeting, stopping directly in front of her. "You can't deny that we've been getting along extremely well lately."

"We have," she admitted reluctantly. "But we're talking about work."

"We weren't working during dinner," Patrick pointed out with maddening logic. He took her hands in his. They were ice cold.

Carly had known from the beginning that Patrick Ryan was going to prove to be trouble and as his thumbs stroked provocative little paths on her palms, she was aware of exactly how dangerous a man he could be when he put his mind to it. As if reading her thoughts, he lifted her wrist to his lips.

The rush of arousal that whipped through Carly was both exhilarating and frightening. She cleared her throat, striving for a cool, composed tone.

"During dinner we were behaving like friends. Let's just keep it that way." She tugged lightly in an attempt to free her hand, but Patrick seemed in no hurry to relinquish possession.

"That's fine with me," he agreed, a smile playing at the corner of his lips. "Exactly how friendly are you feeling tonight?" He pulled her a little closer. "Your pulse is racing, Carly. You're not afraid of me, are you?"

As Patrick's lips hovered inches from hers, his eyes were grave, revealing concern. "Carly?"

It was only her name, but his husky voice seemed to caress it, bestowing a warmth she had never heard before. Carly found herself tempted beyond reason.

"I'm not afraid of you," she answered softly.

His crystal-blue eyes cleared, but remained filled with questions. His brows drew together in concentration as he studied her thoughtfully. When he cupped the back of her neck with his hand, Carly trembled, unprepared for the flash of desire ignited by the touch of his strong fingers on her bare skin. Her mouth went dry.

"You're afraid of something," he diagnosed quietly.

Carly swallowed, finding it did nothing to ease the dryness of her throat. "I'm afraid of myself," she said in a low voice. "I've never wanted to be with a man as much I want to be with you, Patrick, but it's terrifying to have so little control over my feelings."

Patrick was momentarily shaken by her candor. He was not used to experiencing total honesty as a prelude to making love. There were certain initial steps to be taken—little games men and women played to protect themselves, to keep things from becoming too heavy. But if Carly had ever learned those little tricks, she'd obviously disregarded them, opting instead for that distressing candor that should have cooled his passion, but for some unfathomable reason didn't.

"Would it make you feel any safer to know that you've affected me the same way?" He brushed his lips softly against hers.

At the feel of his warm breath wafting across her skin, Carly's knees weakened. "Really?" Her fingers crept into his midnight-black hair.

"Really," Patrick confirmed, his lips moving to the vulnerable hollow of her throat. "I walked into that restaurant more than a week ago anticipating a battle with some cold, calculating career woman who's more comfortable going to bed with her ledger sheets than a man."

Carly's skin tingled as he slipped his hand under her sweater to stroke her naked back. "I'm not at all like that," she argued softly.

His fingers danced down the small, delicate bones of her spine. "I know," he murmured as his lips traced the contours of her ear. "I realized that the moment I looked across that sea of bureaucrats and saw you holding hands with McIntyre."

Carly tilted her head back, attempting to focus on Patrick's face. Her mind was growing hazy; speech took a major effort.

"Patrick, were you actually jealous of Bill?"

He cupped a hand over her breast, pleased by the way she trembled when his thumb scraped against the burgeoning tip. "I wanted to kill the guy."

Carly was stunned by the strength of his tone. "You wouldn't have."

A reluctant humor filled Patrick's eyes. "No," he agreed, punctuating his words with kisses, "I wouldn't have. But that didn't stop me from wanting to. I had an irrational desire to walk over to that table, stake my claim and carry you out— caveman style—over my shoulder."

"I thought cavemen dragged their women around by their hair."

In response, Patrick thrust his hands into her honey tresses, tangling them around his fingers. "Shall we give it a try?"

As he pulled her against him, Carly felt the seductive stirring of her body's response. It built slowly, insistently, evolving into an ache that permeated every cell. Her blood thickened as desire surged through her, seeking a means of release. As he pressed his palms against the back of her thighs, urging her closer still, Carly felt her legs disintegrating from the knees down.

She knew that only by making love with Patrick would she be able to turn this pain to pleasure. But first, there was something she had to know.

"Were you telling me the truth when you promised you'd never lie to me?"

Patrick moved his hips insinuatingly against hers. "Yes."

Carly's question came as a shock to his entire system. "Is your wife the reason you refuse to allow yourself to fall in love again?"

Patrick froze, attempting to decipher the words that rang in his ears, competing with the roar of blood. "Who told you about Julia?"

"That doesn't matter. You promised to tell me the truth, Patrick."

Carly thought she might fall to the Oriental rug underfoot as Patrick's hands dropped to his sides. "I don't want to talk about her. . . . My God, woman, your timing is not to be believed!"

"I'm waiting for an answer," she prompted softly.

Patrick turned away from her gentle gaze. "It doesn't have anything to do with us," he insisted, his low words sounding false even to his own ears.

Carly couldn't help but be affected by the pain in Patrick's tone. Unable to resist, she spanned the slight distance between them and looped her arms around his waist as she pressed her cheek against his tense back.

"Yes, it does, Patrick," she insisted in a low, fervent voice. "It has everything to do with us. And no matter how strongly you deny it, you know that it's true."

Patrick took Carly's breath away as he spun around, a fierce look on his face. Then slowly, like the cracking of a plaster mold, his anger fell away, leaving in its place an expression of resigned acceptance.

He stroked the planes of her face with trembling fingers. "What is it about you?" he asked in tones of wonder. "Why can't I resist you? Is it magic, Carly?" His thumbnail outlined her lips. "Are you a sorceress? A witch, perhaps?"

He lowered his mouth to hers, slowly savoring the sweetness of her lips. Conflict raged within him—he wanted to pull her to the floor and quench these fires burning within him, never mind the consequences. But Carly was a woman who should be treated tenderly. Some distant part of Patrick's mind cautioned restraint, even as he realized that once he had made love to her, there would be no turning back.

Carly's lips were mobile under his—tasting, teasing, offering untold delights. So many secrets, she thought through the golden, shimmering light flooding her mind. He was not a man to give himself to love easily. As she closed her eyes to the blissful feel of his mouth on hers, his hands skimming over her body, Carly knew that whatever Patrick might answer, she would love him. She had no choice in the matter. The dictates of her heart had already decreed her fate.

"It doesn't matter," she whispered as she tugged his shirt loose. Her hands fretted against the warm, moist skin of his back.

Patrick's arms tightened convulsively around her, and he buried his lips into the fragrant skin of her neck. "I can't wait for you any longer."

Carly framed his face with her palms. "I don't want you to," she answered simply. Her wide eyes darkened with desire. "Is this where you drag me off by my hair?"

He hooked an arm behind her knees, lifting her up against his chest. "I'm afraid you'll have to settle for being carried off to bed, sweetheart. Civilization does have its drawbacks, after all."

Carly's smile was beatific as she twined her arms about his neck. "I've always wanted to be swept off my feet."

When Patrick lowered Carly to his bed, she turned molten under his hands, yielding even as she took. His entire body aching for release, Patrick murmured words of love—mad promises that he could never hope to keep but longed for, from the depths of his soul.

Clothes seemed to disintegrate, blown away by the whirlwind of their passion. Patrick touched her everywhere, causing her body to hum with an electric awareness. In turn, as Carly's delicate hands explored his body without shame, she exulted in the way she could bring him pleasure.

Patrick's entire being flamed with a volatile, dangerous passion that threatened to consume him. Her slender body was fluid under his, her skin warm under his fingertips. Carly expelled a soft sigh of pleasure as his roving hand moved between the satin of her thighs.

"You're so warm," he murmured in tones of wonder. "So ready for me. Tell me," he insisted gruffly. "Tell me you want me."

Carly lifted her hips against his touch. "Oh, Patrick, can't you tell?"

"I need to hear the words." Patrick stroked her intimately, provocatively, his fingers seeking out the hidden places of her body. "Don't hold back from me, Carly," he murmured achingly. "Not tonight."

Mesmerized by the extent of Patrick's need, Carly slid her hand down his chest, her fingers teasing in the crisp pelt of hair. Patrick groaned as her exploring hand moved lower still, encountering the rigid strength of his maleness. Her fingers curled around him.

"I need you, Patrick," she managed in a ragged tone, enthralled as he thrust against her intimate touch. "Please, make love to me."

Patrick needed no further invitation. As he poised over Carly, he paused, wanting to remember everything about this moment of possession for the rest of his life. Her hair was spread out on the pillow like spilled gold, her forehead was beaded with glistening beads of moisture, her bottom lip was caught between perfect white teeth, and her eyes—God, those lovely, lovely eyes—were darkly laced with such passion that his body throbbed with an answering need.

"Yes," Carly said softly.

Unable to wait another moment, Patrick surged forward, a red mist burning before his eyes as she lifted her hips, taking him deep inside her.

Carly's self-control had been hanging by a slender thread, but as Patrick began to move, it snapped, flinging her into a furnace of blazing hunger. Her nails scraped the skin of his back, and her hands roamed the rippling muscles as she gave herself fully to a force more powerful, more primitive, than anything she had ever known. She was dimly aware of Patrick saying her name, over and over again, whether in victory or surrender she could not discern.

But then the flames built up inside her—higher, then higher still—and as fire ripped through her body and heat overwhelmed her mind, Carly's last coherent thought was of Patrick. How desperately she loved him.

Afterward, as they lay in a tangle of arms and legs, neither spoke. Patrick was thinking how fully, how freely Carly had given herself to him. How she had held nothing back, surrendering completely. But who had actually done the surrendering, he wondered. And which of them had emerged the victor?

While Patrick attempted to sort out his thoughts, Carly mentally held her breath. In the cooling aftermath of their lovemaking, she viewed her behavior more clearly. She hadn't meant to force the issue of Patrick's past, but ever since

Alex had told her the tragic story, the only thing she could think about was how to comfort him. How to make up for his loss. In offering herself to him, she had sought to get past the barriers he had erected between them, allowing their relationship to blossom freely, without the burdens of past sorrows.

But even then he had held back, keeping his secrets locked deep inside him. Carly wondered if he would ever let down his defenses and allow himself to love again. It was all too soon, she considered now, mutely shaking her head. The slight gesture caught Patrick's attention and he looked down at her, but Carly turned her head away.

"No," he insisted quietly, turning her troubled face back toward him. "It's too late to hide now, Carly. It's too late for either of us." His touch was gentle as he smoothed the long damp strands of hair from her forehead. "I want to look at you."

"I'm sorry if I hurt you by bringing up your wife, Patrick," Carly whispered, lifting a hand to his cheek. She swallowed, her eyes eloquent in her need to make him understand. "I wanted to make love with you so very, very much."

Despite her penchant for honesty, Carly refrained from telling Patrick of her love. She had already gambled too much and now feared the risk of losing him completely.

Patrick propped himself up on one elbow, drinking in the sight of her. When he stroked her breast, Carly closed her eyes to his exquisite touch, and when his lips lowered to brush against her flesh, she could feel the warmth of his slight sigh.

"Carly, Carly," he mused out loud, his hands more gentle now that his hunger had been temporarily satiated. "What am I going to do with you?"

Slowly, lazily, she opened her eyes and gave him a tender smile. "I've a few ideas along that line," she invited, pressing her palm against his chest.

Patrick felt an immediate stirring in his loins and was both amazed and thrilled that he could want her so badly so soon again. There would be time enough for thinking, he decided. Later.

"I'm always open for suggestions," he drawled. "What would you say to sharing a shower with me?"

"I'd say yes," she agreed instantly, punctuating her words with light kisses against his smiling lips.

"And then I want you back in my bed. All night."

Carly tilted her head back, her bright eyes lit with an enticing mingling of desire and humor. "Yes."

11

PATRICK AWOKE FIRST. He spent several pleasurable minutes watching Carly sleep, the sight of her imbuing him with an inexplicable sense of tenderness. Her lips were curved in a slight smile, and when he couldn't resist the temptation to trace them with his fingertip, Carly's eyelids immediately fluttered open. At first, she seemed disoriented by the strange surroundings; her dark blue irises were slightly veiled. As her eyes met his they cleared, and she smiled in warm remembrance.

"Good morning."

He bent his head to kiss her. "Good morning."

Carly couldn't remember ever being so happy. She stretched luxuriously. "What time is it?"

Patrick was idly playing with her hair, sifting the golden strands through his fingers like grains of sand. "Late. It's almost time to leave for the office."

"Have you been awake long?"

As he arranged her hair over her shoulders, the heels of his hands lightly massaged her breasts. He could feel her tremble under the intimate touch.

"A few minutes."

Carly trailed a fingernail down the center of his torso. "You should have wakened me."

"I was enjoying watching you sleep."

"That couldn't have been much fun," she protested, moving her palm across his taut, flat stomach.

At Patrick's quick intake of breath, Carly experienced a rush of feminine pride that she could affect him so harshly with a mere touch.

"On the contrary, I can't remember when I've enjoyed anything more. You're beautiful, Carly Ashton."

Patrick leaned down to kiss the peak of her breast. "Absolutely exquisite."

"How late are we?"

He settled over her, moving in such a way that the friction between their bodies seemed to create sparks in the predawn darkness of the bedroom. "Not *that* late," Patrick answered, slipping into her with a slow, smooth motion.

IT WAS A LONG WHILE before Carly emerged from the seductive trance. She pressed her lips experimentally against Patrick's warm, moist skin. He tasted wonderful. Dark and musky, with a piquant tang of salt. He tasted like a man. Her man, she thought happily.

As she stirred in his arms, Patrick stroked her back, his fingers rippling down the delicate bones of her spine. Carly's slender body appeared so fragile that he had been afraid of hurting her, of breaking her as one might damage a piece of fine porcelain. But she possessed a resilient strength that had both surprised and thrilled him. She hadn't backed down from him in the office and she'd proved over and over again last night that her passions ran as deep and as strong as his.

Carly was neither an easy nor pliant woman; she would never remain passive, merely accepting whatever he offered. She was nothing like Julia, he considered reflectively, experiencing a slight stab of guilt for what he vaguely felt to be an unfaithful thought. He had made love to several women before his marriage, as well as a good many after Julia's death. Yet none had ever stimulated such introspection.

He had always been forthright about his lack of commitment; his relationships had always been based solely on mutual physical pleasure. In that respect, his personal life had been satisfactory. If, after passions cooled, Patrick found himself from time to time experiencing disillusionment, or an odd, empty feeling, he would force those thoughts away, concentrating instead on the present.

But Carly was an entirely different matter. She had him contemplating a future even when he knew none existed. Unwilling to dwell on the impossible, he smacked her lightly on the bottom.

"Hey, sleepyhead, it's time to get to work."

"Mmm," she complained drowsily. "I absolutely detest people who can function in the morning."

He chuckled, kissing the top of her head. "I didn't hear any complaints earlier."

Carly lifted her head, her eyes sparkling with humor. "That's different. Besides, you have no idea what lengths I'll go to to avoid getting out of bed in the morning."

Patrick's eyes drank in her slender body, her small, uplifted breasts, her lips that were darkly pink from a night of being thoroughly kissed. "While I'd love to spend the rest of the day making mad, passionate love with you, we *do* have an airline to save."

Carly gave him a look of mock censure. "No wonder you're so successful. Your mind is always on business."

Patrick toyed with a tendril of blond hair that skimmed her shoulders. "Not always."

"Not always," Carly echoed softly, smiling up at him. She pressed a quick kiss against his lips, then exited the bed with a deep sigh. "I always feel more human after my shower," she promised. Halfway to the bathroom she turned, her bright eyes provocative. "Want to come scrub my back?"

Patrick grinned. "I'd love to take you up on that invitation, sweetheart, but I do have to preserve a modicum of energy for the grueling day ahead of us."

"Spoilsport." The smile was still on Carly's lips as she left the bedroom.

Carly was dressed and sipping gratefully on the coffee Patrick had prepared when he entered the kitchen after his own brief shower.

"I have to stop by my apartment and change," she said.

"Fine." He poured himself a cup of coffee. "You can pack while you're at it."

"Pack?"

"I want you to move in with me," Patrick stated casually as he perused the contents of his refrigerator. "We don't have time to cook anything, but there's some juice if you'd like a glass."

Dumbfounded, Carly stared at him. "I can't move in with you, Patrick."

He pulled out a carton of orange juice, pouring some into a glass. "Of course you can. Do you want any of this?"

She lowered her cup to the table. "It's too soon."

Patrick drank the juice without taking his eyes off her. "I'd say it's not soon enough," he countered smoothly.

She frowned. "People will talk."

"Let them."

Carly realized that had been the wrong approach. Patrick would never care about idle gossip. She sought another excuse.

"I'd make a rotten roommate," she argued, staring down at her hands as she toyed nervously with the slender gold band on her finger. "I kick my shoes off the moment I enter a room, I throw my clothes on a chair in the bedroom, and sometimes a week goes by before I get around to hanging them up. I never put the top back on the toothpaste, and you'll have to fight your way past the nylons hanging on the rod to take your shower."

"So we'll hire a housekeeper." He turned away, putting his glass in the dishwasher.

"Then there's my painting; your house will smell like turpentine."

"I'll never notice. When you're in a room, all I can smell is your perfume."

"My taps will ruin your floors."

"We'll cover the scuff marks with rugs."

"I play the stereo too loud. Sometimes in the middle of the night when I stay up to read."

He shrugged uncaringly. "I like music. And besides, you're going to be too occupied at night to care about reading."

With a vast effort, Carly managed to maintain a calm tone. "Is this how you usually handle your affairs?"

Patrick's expression became remote. "I've never asked a woman to live with me, Carly. Not since . . ." He took a deep breath. "Not since I was married," he stated, unable to say Julia's name out loud while his heart was pounding with unaccustomed anxiety.

Carly could feel his tension; it reached out and surrounded her, entering her, infusing itself into her bloodstream as his passion had done the night before. She rose from her chair and crossed the room to stand silently before him, waiting.

Patrick put his arms around her and closed his eyes against the flood of tenderness Carly's act of submission evoked. For a long, silent moment they stood there, each drawing strength from the other.

When she lifted her head, her eyes were clear, but wary. "Why, Patrick?" she asked softly. "Why me? And why now?"

If she was expecting a declaration of love, Carly was to be disappointed. Patrick's mouth was set in a hard line, and his expression displayed a definite lack of joy.

"I don't know," he admitted, wishing he could give Carly what he felt she wanted. "I only know that right now I don't want to live without you." His jaw firmed. "I won't live without you."

Carly knew that admission of need had cost him a great deal. The barriers Patrick had erected around his heart had been years in the building. She couldn't expect them to tumble in a single night. She lifted her hand, her fingertips soothing the muscle that jerked in his dark cheek.

"I'll go home and pack."

Relief, mixed with a warmth that told Carly she had made the right decision, flooded into his eyes. "I'll try not to make you regret this."

"It was my decision to make, Patrick," she reminded him calmly. "I won't regret it."

Patrick's arms stayed around her waist as he walked her out to her car. "I'll see you at the office," he said, bending to give her another long kiss before closing the door. "Oh, and don't forget to toss in a long dress."

"Why?"

"The senator's having a party tonight. I promised I'd be there." He closed his eyes in brief disgust. "You might call it a command performance."

Carly belatedly remembered the phone call from Mrs. Ryan. Patrick certainly hadn't sounded pleased with the idea then, and looking at his granite face, she concluded that his feelings hadn't changed.

"I like parties," she offered with a tentative smile.

She was rewarded as his expression softened slightly. "I don't know why I didn't think of taking you along to run interference years ago. This actually may be one Ryan bash I end up enjoying."

Carly felt an odd twist of pleasure at his words. "We didn't know each other years ago."

He brushed his knuckles along her cheek. "Then we'll just have to begin making up for lost time."

"If I'd known we were going out tonight, Patrick Ryan, I'd have kept you in bed longer this morning." Carly's saucy grin banished the last vestiges of inner conflict from his expression.

Patrick was still chuckling to himself as he reentered the house, gathering up the papers for the long day ahead.

CARLY WAS ENGROSSED in studying the layouts for Capitol's new ad campaign when Patrick appeared in her office doorway later that morning.

"I just had a call from Baker."

She put down her pen. "Any problems we don't already know about?"

He shook his head. "I don't think so. In fact, he agreed to have lunch with me today."

Carly leaned her elbows on her desk, resting her chin on top of her linked fingers. "That sounds as if it might be good news," she suggested tentatively. "I didn't expect to hear from him until next week."

"Neither did I."

"Do you want me to come with you?"

Patrick considered that for a moment. "I don't think you'd better," he decided finally. "Not that I wouldn't appreciate your moral support, but everyone knows how close you are to McIntyre. It's important Baker understand he's dealing with me."

"That makes sense. But I still wish there was something I could do to help."

"You can wish me luck."

A brilliant smile brightened Carly's face. "I can do better than that." She reached into the pocket of her skirt. "Close your eyes and hold out your hand."

Patrick looked wary but did as Carly asked. She placed the penny into his palm, closing his fingers over it.

He opened his eyes, studying the metallic talisman. "What is this?"

"It's my lucky penny. Gramps gave it to me years and years and years ago. It's always brought me luck."

His blue eyes darkened. "You're willing to share it with me?"

Carly's expression displayed all the love she felt for him. "Everything I have is yours, Patrick."

At that moment, Patrick wanted nothing more than to lock the office door and spend the remainder of the day making love to Carly. He sighed as he forced his mind back to the upcoming meeting.

"Thank you, sweetheart. I promise to take good care of it." He brushed a quick kiss against her lips. "I'd better get back to work."

Carly's slight sigh revealed that idea was not her first choice, either. "Me too," she agreed, casting a glance at the paperwork scattered over her desk. She pressed her palm against his cheek. "Good luck."

He grinned, flipping the coin into the air. "With my lady's lucky penny in hand, how can I miss?"

PATRICK HAD CHOSEN the restaurant for the meeting with Warren Baker with care. He had the feeling the union representative would enjoy flaunting his political muscle and the descending staircase of Mel Krupin's ensured that diners would be seen by other equally powerful figures. By the way

Baker's shoulders squared in his navy blue suit, Patrick knew he had guessed right.

A more personal reason for choosing this particular restaurant was that it reminded him of home. The look was New York and the food was New York, right down to the pickles. Here he could pretend, for a while, that he was back in the bustling metropolis he'd adopted nearly twenty years ago. The city where he was accepted on his own merits, not for what his father had done.

Warren Baker had obviously come loaded for bear. The man shot off the opening volley, disallowing Patrick an opportunity to begin the discussion on his own terms.

"I find it damn difficult to understand how you can turn your back on everything your family has stood for," he stated gruffly.

"I haven't."

Baker took a drink of the imported dark beer. "Mike Ryan always supported the unions," he challenged.

"What makes you think I don't?"

The older man arched a steely brow. "Come on, Ryan, give me a break. You're the antithesis of a labor supporter. You've made your career by riding in management's back pocket."

Patrick steepled his fingers together as he met Baker's glare. "It was my background that led me to believe management and unions have to work together for a more productive society."

Baker answered with an unmannerly snort.

"Look," Patrick continued in a low but forceful voice, "our backgrounds are not that dissimilar."

"That's a joke." Baker's gaze raked over Patrick. "Have you ever seen a copper smelter?"

"I have," Patrick answered truthfully. "I negotiated a contract last year for a mine in Utah."

"Then you know it's like hellfire in there. The difference was that once you finished pushing your papers around, you got to leave. A lot of men spend their lives at those furnaces, and the unions are the only breath of fresh air they get."

Baker shot Patrick an accusing look. "You can't possibly know what it's like, Ryan. You grew up filthy rich while I watched my father struggle for every dime he earned."

"And I watched my father struggle to make certain your father won every cent he was entitled to. As well as having a safe environment to work in."

Baker's face still maintained an argumentative expression, but he remained silent.

"Deregulation hurt the airlines," Patrick continued. "They're all drowning in red ink, and it makes a hell of a lot more sense for us to turn our combative spirit loose on the competition instead of each other."

"Sure," Baker growled, "and while we're falling for that line, McIntyre crushes the unions and gets rid of the contracts."

Patrick's knuckles whitened as he pressed his fingers more firmly together, but his expression remained calm.

"I've already told you, you're not dealing with McIntyre. You're dealing with me."

"Are you telling me McIntyre isn't in the wings, waiting for you to con us out of our benefits?" Baker accused heatedly.

Patience had never been one of Patrick's strong suits. Reminding himself of all that was at stake, he struggled to keep his temper in check.

"I'm not saying McIntyre isn't returning to Capitol. But for the time being, he's taken a leave of absence. The board has given me full bargaining power and any contract I negotiate will be upheld, no matter what happens down the road."

Baker took another long drink of beer, considering Patrick's words. "I think you're telling the truth," he said finally.

"That's a start." Patrick began to relax. "These are difficult times for all of us," he said. "Management is struggling, but you have to admit that labor is also suffering a profound crisis. What it comes down to, Baker, is that unions are either going to be elite protectionist societies for a hierarchy of workers, or they'll move forward by becoming involved with issues like management and productivity."

"Hell, don't you think I know the old ways aren't working?" Baker ground out. "Sure, it sounds good, but how do you propose to make it work?"

"Enabling workers to own stock in the companies is the first step. We have to face the fact that we're all in this together. We all want to put food on our tables, money in our pockets and go home with a sense that we've done a fair day's work for a fair day's pay." Patrick shrugged, taking a drink of his own beer. "In that respect labor isn't any different from any other person trying to earn a living."

Baker was thoughtful for a moment. "How'd you say we get the money to buy in?"

Sensing the change in attitude, Patrick allowed himself a fleeting sense of exhilaration.

"It's not as difficult as it sounds. The unions use bank loans to purchase shares in the company, which they distribute to the workers as additional benefits."

Baker rubbed his jaw. "And we'd have a say in management decisions?"

"Like any other group of owners."

"Management would have to cut its head count," the union representative warned. "You can't expect us to take losses, without giving up your nonessential personnel."

"Agreed," Patrick said instantly, having already determined the cuts Capitol could make without hindering its operation. He pulled a pen from his jacket pocket. "What else?"

They spent the next two hours going over the details of the contract, item by item. By the time Patrick returned to the office, he felt optimistic that when Baker took the offer to his negotiating board, the vote would be unanimous for ratification.

CARLY HAD BEEN TRYING to work, but her mind kept drifting across town to where the all-important meeting was taking place. Her spirits lifted when Patrick came striding into her office, whistling happily. He tossed her the penny.

"I've never believed in lucky charms before today."

She rose from her desk, coming to greet him. "It went well," she guessed.

"What would you say if I told you that we're looking at wage cuts of twenty percent, reductions in medical, dental and vacation benefits, as well as additional flying time per crew?"

She leaned back against her desk, crossing her arms over her red jacket. "I'd say you're either a magician, or you spent the lunch hour giving away the store."

Patrick grinned, his eyes twinkling. "Would you consider handing over a twenty-five percent stake in Capitol, giving the unions representation on the board, plus increased involvement in all aspects of decision making—with the exception of wallpaper and paint colors, of course—giving away the store?"

Carly stared at him. That was precisely what Patrick had wanted all along, but only she had known that. He really was a wizard, she considered.

"Are they really going to ratify?"

He nodded. "I believe so."

Carly flung her arms around his neck, kissing him soundly on the mouth. "Even for a white knight, you're absolutely amazing!"

"That's what I've been telling you." He tilted his head back, eyeing her tentatively. "Uh, there was one other little matter I forgot to mention."

"Oh? What was that?" she asked absently, nibbling at the lobe of his ear.

"I know we hadn't discussed the possibility ahead of time, but at the last minute talks started breaking down and I had to come up with something to throw in the pot. I hope it won't prove too much of a loss."

His suddenly serious tone caught her attention. "What did you promise Warren Baker, Patrick?"

"I had to agree to marry his daughter. It seems she's been eating him out of house and home for years while she waits for some handsome fella to come riding up on a white charger and carry her off." Patrick grinned. "Apparently we white knights are a bit difficult to find in this day and age."

Carly punched him on the arm. "You scared me to death, Patrick Ryan!"

"Ow!" He rubbed his sleeve. "For a skinny thing, you pack one helluva punch, lady."

"It's the juggling. It builds upper arm strength."

"Interesting," he mused. "You are a very versatile woman, Carly Ashton. Do you have any other hidden talents I have yet to uncover?"

"A few."

Patrick gave her a friendly leer. "How about giving me a demonstration, once we get home?"

In response, Carly picked her purse up from the corner of the desk, pulled her coat and hat from the brass rack and slipped her arm through his.

"That's the best offer I've had all day," she stated happily, reaching behind her to flick off the light as they left the office.

12

TWO HOURS LATER, Patrick was leaning against the bathroom doorframe, watching Carly prepare for the party at his parents' Chevy Chase home. Her frantic energy reminded him of a whirling dervish as she raced back and forth between the bedroom and the bathroom, digging into suitcases and shopping bags, searching for the items of female paraphernalia she'd carelessly packed.

"I know it's in here somewhere," she muttered, delving into a brown paper bag in an attempt to locate her eyeliner.

"You've looked everywhere else," he agreed. "Which was no small feat considering how many trips it took me to haul in all your stuff."

She shot him a withering glance. "I warned you that I didn't travel light."

"I wasn't complaining, sweetheart," Patrick assured her amiably. "However, I will admit to being amazed at how much you managed to squeeze into a 1983 Mustang."

"It's a hatchback," she murmured, as if that explained everything. "Aha!" She pulled out the gray pencil with a victorious flourish. "Success."

Leaning over the bathroom sink, she drew a quick, deft line along each lid, smudging the corners to give her eyes a slightly smoky appearance. When she caught Patrick's amused gaze in the mirror, she frowned.

"Why are you wasting time grinning at me like that? You're not nearly ready."

"Men don't take much time," he informed her negligently. "A quick shower, a change of clothes, that's about it. Besides, it's a lot more fun watching you try to keep that towel up."

Carly glanced down at the bath towel that had slipped down around her waist. She rewrapped it around her bared breasts, shooting him an angry look.

"Voyeur."

His grin widened. "And enjoying every minute of it. You don't have to worry, you know. Nobody ever shows up at a party on time. It's much better to be fashionably late."

She brushed some wine blush along her cheekbones. "I don't like being late."

"So I'm discovering. It's a fascinating contradiction, really. The prompt, efficient career woman and the delightfully disorganized nymph."

"I think that was a sexist remark," Carly complained with a smile. "Besides, for your information, Patrick Ryan, I have a very compartmentalized mind. I can separate my business life from my personal life."

Seeing his brightening gaze, she tugged more tightly on the towel. "And we wouldn't be running so late if you hadn't insisted on ravishing my body the minute we walked in the door."

"Is that a complaint? I don't remember you fighting me off."

Carly's eyes softened with the memory of their recent lovemaking. "Of course it's not," she assured him instantly. "I was simply stating a fact."

She brushed on a light dusting of violet eye shadow, then gave her lashes a quick sweep with mascara. "Done. Now all I have to do is get dressed."

She moved past him on the way back into the bedroom. "It's all yours," she said, tossing her head toward the bathroom.

"I'll try to fight my way through the rubble."

Carly spun around, her fists on her scantily covered hips. "When I have time to put everything properly in its place, I will," she informed him archly. "For now, Patrick, you'll have to suffer."

Unable to resist the fire in her eyes, as well as the way her challenging gesture had jerked the towel down once again, Patrick responded with a slow, lazy smile. His arms encircled her waist and as Carly instantly relented, her own arms encircling his neck, the skimpy towel fell unheeded to the floor.

"I'm glad you're here," he said, brushing his lips lightly against hers.

How amazing that those simple words could give her such pleasure, Carly considered. But everything about Patrick made her feel as if the world had been born anew. As she closed her eyes to the sweetness of his kiss, Carly whispered, "Me too."

It was not a kiss of gentle exploration, nor was it laced with the passion they'd shared so often in their short time together. Instead, his lips seemed to be promising a lifetime of such kisses, and Carly was disappointed when it came to an end much too quickly.

"I forgot my dress." She slipped out of his arms and returned to the bathroom. "Oh, damn," she groaned as she took the plum silk dress from where she'd hung it on the towel rack. "I'd hoped the wrinkles would steam out when I took my shower."

At the haphazard way Carly had tossed her clothing into the mismatched suitcases, Patrick doubted that a year of showers would have managed that feat.

"Finish getting ready," he suggested. "I'll press it for you."

"You? Really? I never would have imagined you to be the domestic type, Patrick."

He winked, plucking the dress from her hands. "I have my moments."

True to his word, Patrick not only salvaged Carly's dress, but was in and out of the shower in a flash and met her in the living room looking unreasonably handsome in his formal evening wear.

"You look wonderful," she stated as he entered the room. Chewing thoughtfully on a fingernail, Carly studied him from the top of his dark head down to the shiny black dress shoes.

"There's just one thing missing." She pulled the silk handkerchief from his breast pocket.

"Hey, it took me five minutes to get that thing folded right!"

Ignoring Patrick's complaint, Carly opened the silk square with a flick of her wrist, displaying a white rose.

"How did you do that?" Patrick asked as she pinned it to his lapel.

"Magic," Carly replied serenely. She replaced the handkerchief and nodded her head approvingly. "There. Now you look absolutely perfect. You know, Patrick, you should always wear a tuxedo."

"Wouldn't work," he argued amiably. "I'd have to change careers and although I've always considered myself a brilliant financier, I think I'd make a rotten headwaiter."

Patrick smiled as he studied Carly with a slow, leisurely perusal. He couldn't remember ever seeing anything quite so lovely. She had piled her thick hair atop her head, securing it with a pair of mother-of-pearl trimmed combs. The plum silk halter dress allowed a weakening glimpse of her creamy shoulders and the dark color brought out the unique hue of her eyes. The dress was deceptively simple, falling from her throat to her feet in smooth, graceful lines, but the way the silk hugged her curves had him wishing all the more that he'd never agreed to this evening.

"Let's stay home," he said suddenly.

Despite the obvious desire in his gaze, Carly felt Patrick had other reasons for avoiding the Ryan party. "You promised to go."

His mouth firmed. "I know. Only because I know damn well that if Mohammed won't come to the mountain, the mountain will show up here."

His grim tone led Carly to believe Senator Ryan's presence would not be welcome in Patrick's home, and she was beginning to wonder what she'd gotten herself into. She had never met anyone in Washington who didn't have a good thing to say about Senator Mike Ryan, even those who'd continually found themselves on the other side of the political fence. Yet she was getting the distinct impression that he had one very strong detractor. His son.

"Let's go." Patrick abruptly took her arm and practically hauled her out the door.

He remained silent while driving, responding to Carly's attempts at conversation with a few muttered monosyllables. Finally giving up, she fell silent. The air in the car seemed to vibrate with ill humor, which was all the more reason she was surprised when Patrick suddenly turned to her at a stoplight.

"Did I tell you that you look exceptionally beautiful tonight, Ms Ashton?"

"No," she stated shortly, turning to gaze out the window. She heard Patrick sigh. He reached out and cupped her chin with his fingers, returning her mutinous gaze to his.

"Then I was definitely remiss. You are lovely."

His deep, husky tone invited forgiveness, but Carly wasn't quite ready to give in. "Thank you." Her tone was as frosty as the night air.

"Aren't you talking to me?" That crooked smile she loved hovered at the edges of his lips.

"Of course I am."

"Your dress brings out your violet eyes "

"They're blue."

"They're violet," he corrected softly. "And I hate seeing them unhappy." His palm framed the side of her face. "I didn't mean to take my problems out on you, Carly. Even though I can't promise it won't happen again, I will try."

He looked inclined to say something else when the loud blare of a car horn behind them signaled the light had turned green some time ago. Patrick muttered a soft oath, casting an angry glance up at the rearview mirror.

Carly patted his leg. "You're forgiven. Besides, I was behaving a little foolishly myself."

Ignoring the insistent demand from the other driver, Patrick covered her hand with his. "It won't be easy," he said with sudden seriousness. "Neither of us is used to sharing space. There are bound to be conflicts."

Carly had known that; she just hadn't wanted to face the fact so soon. "We'd better go."

He glanced up at the traffic light. "We can't. It just turned red again." His gaze, when it returned to her, was unnervingly solemn. "We're both strong-minded individuals, Carly. We're bound to fight from time to time. Let's at least agree to try not to hurt each other while we're together."

She couldn't help herself. The words were out of her mouth before she had a chance to censor them. "And how long will that be?" she asked quietly.

Patrick's eyes shadowed in the spreading glow of the streetlight. "I don't know."

Carly searched her mind for a response to that unwelcome admission and came up empty. She felt a flood of relief when the traffic light suddenly turned green. Giving in to the irate driver who'd once again begun pounding on his horn, Patrick shifted gears and stepped on the accelerator.

They took their place in the long line of cars, submitting to a security check before being allowed to continue on to the house, where Senator and Victoria Ryan had arranged for valet parking.

Patrick's mother greeted them at the door, her eyes skimming over Carly with apparent surprise before she tilted her cheek to Patrick.

"Patrick, darling," she scolded lightly, "you're late."

"Better late than never, Mother," he responded cheerfully, bending to brush a dutiful kiss against Victoria's lightly rouged cheek.

"Tell that to your father," Victoria warned. Her tone assured Patrick that his mother was, as usual, in the senator's corner when it came to their only son's career choices.

He mumbled a reply, but Victoria had turned her attention toward Carly. "Miss Ashton," she stated with a smile, "we've met before."

"Yes, several times," Carly agreed. "I believe the last was when I did a benefit performance for those Korean orphans you were sponsoring. It's good to see you again, Mrs. Ryan."

"It's always a pleasure to see you too, dear," Victoria murmured distractedly. "Oh, no," she complained, "there it goes again."

Both Patrick and Carly merely gave her a questioning glance.

"The garage door," Victoria explained. "It seems to be on the same frequency as the secret service walkie-talkies. Every time the men talk to one another, that stupid door opens and closes."

Though she appeared quite distressed by the event, Carly had lived in Washington long enough to know it was a sign of political power to have your television signals and garage doors hampered by such things. After all, it wasn't everyone who had secret service agents roaming the grounds of their home.

In other cities, wealth was the key to social success, but in Washington political power was the sole measure of social standing. Your blood could flow as blue as the upper square on the American flag and your ancestors might have arrived on the *Mayflower*, but to be ensured of a listing in The Green Book, the city's social register, one must get elected to the presidency, Congress or secure an appointment as a Supreme Court justice or Cabinet secretary.

"I noticed the extra manpower," Patrick remarked. "Who rates all the attention?"

Victoria beamed with her success as a socialite. "The president's visiting," she revealed. "I know he'll be delighted to talk with you, Patrick."

She did not have to explain that it was not the current commander in chief who was paying a social call on the Ryan household. As far as Carly knew, no Republican president had ever set foot in the Ryan home. She wondered if Patrick's choice of a career in business had proved disappointing for the liberally oriented family. Perhaps that explained his discomfort.

"I can't imagine why," Patrick responded dryly.

Victoria's laugh was forced. "Modesty doesn't agree with you, dear. You know the president has always enjoyed hearing of your exploits in the world of high finance. Meanwhile, your father is pacing the library floor, waiting to speak with you." Her eyes held little seeds of worry and Patrick knew his mother was afraid he'd trigger the senator's renowned Irish temper.

Giving her son one last warning look, Victoria linked her arm through Carly's. "Come with me, dear. We'll get you circulating while my son and the senator have their little chat."

An hour later, Carly had yet to catch a glimpse of the former president, although she had traded cocktail party conversation with two congressmen, a former secretary of state and one of the few remaining liberals on the Supreme Court who assured the group of party faithfuls surrounding him that he was too ornery to die and allow a conservative to be appointed in his place.

She had sipped the same glass of champagne all evening, and, finally escaping a diatribe about human rights in El Salvador, made her way to a buffet table that groaned with enough food to feed half the Third World. She was in the process of deciding how much of the elaborate fare she could put on her plate without appearing greedy when Alex suddenly appeared beside her.

"Do you suppose the caviar is actually Russian?" he asked under his breath.

Carly grinned, pleased to see a friend. "If it is, you can be certain it'll make headlines in tomorrow's *Post*. 'Senator Ryan soft on communism,'" she quoted blithely.

Alex's dark eyes twinkled attractively before scanning the room. "Where's Patrick?"

"Still with the senator, I imagine," she murmured, piling several slices of smoked ham on her plate, eschewing the caviar altogether. She had never developed a taste for it, despite seven years spent attending Washington parties where it appeared to be de rigueur.

"I haven't heard any shouting yet," Alex offered. "One of those hardheaded Irishmen must be mellowing."

"The president is with them. Do you see any mustard?"

"Right here." Alex handed her a crystal bowl. "The president? The old man is definitely pulling out the heavy artillery."

"Heavy artillery?" She frowned down at the dark mustard heavily laced with horseradish. "Why doesn't anyone ever serve the good old-fashioned yellow kind?"

"Because most individuals invited to these bashes don't have your plebeian tastes," he countered. "Didn't Patrick tell you why this party was thrown together at the last minute?"

Carly decided to forego condiments altogether and stacked the ham onto a slice of rye bread. "I assume it was because the president's in town," she answered. "How's the turkey?"

"Dry. But the smoked salmon is good. And the president being in town is only part of the reason."

"Really?" she asked absently, passing up the turkey in favor of the salmon. She plucked a giant shrimp from its bed of crushed ice, then on further consideration took two more.

"My God, doesn't Patrick feed you?"

"We've been busy working." She added a poppy-seed roll to the mountain of food accumulating on her plate.

"My mother is going to love you," Alex stated with a bold, self-satisfied grin. "There's nothing she loves better than feeding people." His bright eyes took a teasing tour of her slender frame. "Although, I warn you, Carly, she'll do her best to fatten you up. You don't look as if you could supply her with a steady stream of grandchildren."

"Good Lord," Carly complained lightly, "now we're talking about having children. I don't know why I let you talk me into this, Alex."

"It was a fair trade," he reminded her.

Carly's laughing eyes softened. "It was," she agreed.

"So how are things going?"

Before Carly could answer, Patrick appeared. "Just the lady I've been looking for. How would you feel about dancing with a man who just turned his back on a senate seat?"

The pieces of the puzzle suddenly fitted into place. Carly glanced over at Alex, who nodded confirmation to her silent question.

"Since it's probably the only way I'm going to keep you out of the clutches of all those women who were drooling over you when we arrived, I accept," she replied, handing Alex her plate.

Patrick held Carly's hand as he led her to the dance floor, experiencing a sense of calm when he gathered her into his arms. It had taken every bit of his self-control not to lose his temper when faced with Mike Ryan's stubborn insistence that the state of Massachusetts needed a Ryan in the Senate. With Mike on the verge of retiring, Patrick had been the logical choice to succeed his famous father. The additional urging from the former president hadn't helped matters, but Patrick had continued to refuse their elaborate plans for his life. When he had left the library, he had been filled with a seething irritation.

All those negative feelings disintegrated as Carly fitted herself so superbly into his arms. "You're so good for me," he murmured as they swayed slowly to the music. "Two minutes ago I felt like hitting someone. And now..."

She tilted her head to look up at him. "And now?"

"And now all I want to do is make love to my lady." His arms tightened even more. "I didn't want to wait until we got home to hold you."

Carly smiled. "You must have been reading my mind." She rested her head on his shoulder, sighing happily as their bodies melded together. "I'm glad you're not going to run for your father's Senate seat, Patrick."

"Really? I've always had the impression that the idea of having an affair with a congressman appealed to most women."

Her fingers were playing in the soft curls at the back of his head. "I'm not most women."

Patrick looked down at Carly. He couldn't remember seeing anything so lovely. Desire rose from deep within him, flooding over his feeling of contentment.

"No," he murmured thoughtfully. "You're not. You are definitely one of a kind, Carly Ashton."

WINTER SNOWS GAVE WAY to March winds as Carly and Patrick worked to save the airline. On the heels of the pilots' acceptance of Capitol's latest offer, the machinists voted to accept the new offer. All signs pointed to the fact that the attendants' union would follow suit.

Three weeks after moving into Patrick's house, Carly worked a benefit for the World Hunger Council. Knowing that Patrick was in the audience heightened Carly's enjoyment of the evening. She laughed merrily as he badgered her all the way home.

"Tell me how you made that Ethiopian representative disappear in full view of everyone."

"I told him one of your jokes."

"Come on, Carly," he coaxed. "You can tell me." He lifted his right hand as if taking a pledge. "I promise not to confess to anyone how you did it. They can torture me, they can hang me by my toenails, they can even offer me a thousand shares of IBM stock—I promise, my lips are sealed."

"A thousand shares? That's a great deal of money."

"It'd be worth it to find out how you made that guy vanish into thin air."

"Really, Patrick," Carly protested laughingly as they entered the house, "you might as well give up. A magician never reveals her secrets."

"Never?" he asked, reaching out to unbutton her velvet jacket. He tossed it uncaringly onto a chair.

"Never."

Her red silk blouse was next. "Hmm," Patrick murmured, stroking her arms, "nothing up your sleeves. Let's explore a little farther."

He tugged on the zipper of her floor-length skirt, and Carly sucked in her breath as his fingers curved about the waistband. Patrick knelt, drawing the black velvet skirt down her body. When he rose to take her in his arms, she shivered with anticipation.

"Are you sure I can't coax one little secret from you?" His lips feathered a tender trail over her shoulders as he slipped the straps of the lacy camisole down her arms.

"Very sure," Carly whispered, clinging to him as his kisses warmed her skin.

"We'll see about that," Patrick stated decisively. Lifting her into his arms, he headed for the bedroom.

It wasn't long before Carly would have told Patrick anything. But, intent on loving her, he forgot to ask.

A FEW DAYS LATER, Carly received a telephone call from Bill.

"Meredith walked today," he shouted with enthusiasm over the long distance wire. "She had braces on, and it was only a few steps, but by God, she did it on her own, Carly!"

Carly smiled, unreasonably taking Bill's good fortune as an omen. "That's wonderful," she enthused. "When are you bringing her back to Washington?"

"In a few days," he assured her. "I'm looking forward to getting back into harness. Ryan has done a bang-up job; thanks to him I've got something to come home to. Didn't I tell you he was one helluva miracle worker?"

"He is special," Carly concurred softly.

"Well, see you in a few days, sugar."

"A few days," she echoed.

Carly's hand trembled as she hung up the telephone. Despite her pleasure at the thought of Bill returning to work, his arrival could only mean one thing. Patrick's work was concluded. Very soon, perhaps within days, he'd be on his way back to New York. What on earth was she going to do once he had gone?

Lost in her unhappy thoughts, Carly didn't hear Patrick enter her office. She was startled to see him suddenly standing over her.

"Is something wrong?" he asked, seeing her downcast expression.

Carly forced a smile. "Not at all. Meredith is much better. Bill's bringing her home soon. But I suppose you knew that."

"I knew he was coming back to work," Patrick agreed casually. "I didn't know about his daughter. I'm glad, Carly. For Meredith and for the McIntyres. But mostly I'm happy for you."

Carly couldn't have stopped the next words from coming if she had tried. "I love you, Patrick."

Patrick stiffened perceptibly. "Carly—" His voice dropped off as he searched her candid gaze. "I don't know what to say."

Knowing that her confession made him uneasy, Carly only loved him more for not taking the easy way out. He hadn't lied, professing a love he was not yet able to give.

She rose from her chair and brushed a light kiss against his lips. "Then don't say anything," she advised. "Don't worry, Patrick, it's not the end of the world. In fact, if you'd relax a little, you might even find yourself enjoying the experience."

Gathering up some papers, Carly headed toward her office door. "I've got a meeting with the caterers."

When he didn't answer, she glanced back over her shoulder. Patrick appeared strangely shell-shocked. "Patrick," she coaxed on a slight sigh, "don't worry. I promise not to take advantage of you." She put on her coat, preparing to leave.

"I really do have to go. My meeting is across town and I've got only fifteen minutes to get there. You know how I hate being late."

"Will you be back?"

Patrick hated to see Carly leave. Not that he had any suitable answer to her remarkable declaration, but it didn't seem proper to profess one's love, then go dashing off to a meeting to discuss frozen food.

"I don't think so. It may run late."

"I'll see you at home then," he agreed absently. "Carly?"

She turned back again. "Yes, Patrick?"

"Want to go out for dinner tonight? Someplace romantic with violins and candlelight?" That, at least, he could do.

She studied him for a moment. "If it's romance you have in mind, I'd rather share a pizza in bed."

As always, Carly's honesty disarmed Patrick. "I thought you promised not to take advantage."

She flashed him a brilliant grin. "I lied," she professed airily, tossing him a kiss. "So sue me."

The bemused expression remained on Patrick's face long after Carly had left the office and he had returned to work.

13

CARLY'S ADMISSION OF LOVE, rather than complicating their relationship, seemed to smooth the turbulent waters. She and Patrick continued to work well together, but there was a subtle difference in their relationship outside the office. Patrick relaxed in her company, finding her unpredictable, unconventional and constantly delightful.

While she did not discard her optimistic outlook toward life when at work, she managed to temper it with a pragmatism and intelligence he admired more with each passing day. At home, however, Carly allowed her emotions to flow freely and her enthusiasm and unselfish love filled the Georgetown house with warm sunshine.

Patrick grew accustomed to working evenings in the den, listening to the inventive sounds of jazz accompanied by the brisk, metallic tap of her shoes against the parquet floors.

Once she had settled in, Patrick found that Carly wasn't actually messy, just charmingly disorganized. She had a habit of losing her house keys on a daily, often hourly, basis. Not that he minded. The view, as she searched frantically under the bed each morning, was a terrific way to begin the day.

While Patrick was reflecting how easily Carly fitted into his life, she was observing the same thing. Though he was admittedly more reserved than she, instead of finding him stuffy, Carly thought of Patrick as an anchor, a steadying force in her life.

He seemed unperturbed by her choice of music, even though his own record collection consisted mainly of classical music and Broadway show tunes. He never said a word about the scuff marks on the expensive flooring, although she did her best to remember to replace the Oriental rug at the end of each session so as not to call attention to the havoc she was wreaking on his floors. As a special surprise, he had returned to her apartment for her paintings and the bright splashes of color hung in every room, startling against the subdued oyster silk wallpaper.

There had only been one instance when Patrick lost patience. Carly had spent the better part of a Saturday afternoon searching for a misplaced tube of oil paint. She remembered bringing it home from the art supply store. But then she and Patrick had decided to take in a Woody Allen movie and by the time they returned home from dinner and the show, both were eager to go to bed. Carly completely forgot the misplaced paint.

The next morning she was lying in bed, drowsily contemplating the lazy Sunday ahead when there was a roar from the bathroom.

"Carly!"

Leaping up, she raced toward the bathroom, certain Patrick was in peril. Perhaps he had fallen in the shower and hit his head. Or accidentally swallowed the contact lenses that she'd left floating in the glasses filled with solution, unwilling to take the time to locate her storage case the night before. Was soaking solution toxic? She'd never forgive herself if she had poisoned him. Or perhaps, horror of horrors, he had cut his throat shaving.

"Dear God," she prayed under her breath, "please let me remember my first-aid training!"

But when she flung open the door, Patrick bore no sign of injury. The glasses of liquid were still intact on the counter and not a drop of blood darkened his throat. Only the dangerous glitter in his eyes pointed to the fact that something was drastically wrong.

"Patrick," she gasped, her hand against her heart as she fought for breath, "what on earth is the matter?"

He thrust his toothbrush under her nose. "Look at this!"

Carly viewed the bristles covered with cerulean-blue paint. "You found it!" she exclaimed, flinging her arms around his neck. "How wonderful, darling. I thought it had disappeared forever."

As he surrendered to Carly's rewarding kiss, Patrick decided that there were far worse things in life than blue teeth.

A LITTLE MORE than a week after Bill's telephone call, Carly was busy drafting a press release regarding Capitol's much improved status when Patrick entered her office, looking incredibly smug.

"I've got a surprise for you," he announced.

She put down her pen. "You're actually taking me out to lunch." Carly had tried to coax Patrick into lunch away from the office on more than one occasion, but he had steadfastly declined, stating that he couldn't take the time.

"Better than that."

"I've always been a sucker for sapphires."

His eyes twinkled. "Next time," he promised.

"So my surprise is somewhere between a chef salad and a sapphire necklace," she mused. "Is it bigger than a breadbox?"

"Yep."

"Animal, vegetable or mineral?"

"Animal."

A worried frown furrowed her brow. "Patrick, I do hope you didn't bring me anything that needs to be housebroken."

"Is that any way to talk about an old friend?" a familiar voice boomed from the hallway.

"Bill!"

Carly leaped up from her chair and flew across the room as Bill McIntyre strode through the open door. She was embraced in a huge bear hug that soon had her gasping for breath. When she finally managed to extricate herself, her worried gaze moved from Bill to Patrick.

"Everything's fine." Patrick answered her unspoken question. "I'll leave you two to your reunion. McIntyre, after Carly fills you in on the changes in the Salisbury steak, I'll meet you back in your office."

Bill nodded. "That'll be fine. I'm looking forward to being back in harness."

"I'm glad to hear that," Patrick stated amiably. "With you back at work I might even have time to take my girl out to lunch." He surprised Carly by winking broadly before leaving the office.

"So the rumors drifting their way up to Vermont are true." Bill's gaze, as he looked down into Carly's face was fond, but overtly concerned. "You and Ryan are an item."

"I hope it's more than that," she admitted. Then, distracted by Bill's worried expression, Carly changed the subject. "You have to tell me everything."

"It's all been so incredible, I don't know where to start."

"From the beginning."

The time flew as Carly listened, enraptured, to the details of Meredith's progress. While the doctors were hesitating to predict a full recovery, the prognosis was good. The young woman would be able to walk with only the aid of a cane.

While Carly was thrilled for Meredith, she was just as pleased to see Bill looking more like his old self. His color was good, his face flushed with enthusiasm. But the unnatural hue that had been brought about by his high blood pressure was gone. He seemed to have his life back on track, and for that she was exceedingly grateful.

He caught her looking at him thoughtfully. "I'm doing better than ever."

Carly smiled. "I've already got one man who has the unnerving ability to read my mind, Bill. I don't need another."

Bill waved off her complaint. "Your face has always been an open book, Carly. And speaking of Ryan, I take it things are pretty serious between you two."

She couldn't miss the veiled warning in his tone. "So when do I get to visit Meredith?" she asked with feigned brightness.

"A few weeks. She and Elaine are at the house on Hilton Head.... It's not like you to duck an issue, Carly."

Carly sighed, rising from her chair to pace the room. "It's complicated," she stated finally.

"Do you love him?"

Carly met his questioning gaze with a level one of her own. "More than anything."

Bill crossed the room to where she stood, her hands thrust into the pockets of her softly pleated paisley skirt. "Then you'll make it work, Carly."

Her worry showed in her eyes. "I don't know, Bill. I think this time I might have bitten off more than I can chew."

"Hey, that doesn't sound like the Carly Ashton I know and love," he professed. "Granted, Patrick Ryan is reputed to be a tough nut to crack." His gaze was warm with paternal affection. "But you're one in a million, sugar. The man would have to be an idiot to let you get away. And from what Patrick has done to turn Capitol around, that description obviously doesn't fit."

"Then you know what's been going on?"

"He's kept me up to date. Except for one thing." Bill frowned. "Who is that pretty young thing sitting at Marge's desk? And where in the blue blazes is Marge?"

"That pretty young thing is your new secretary, Karla Summers. Patrick promoted Marge to operations." Expecting an argument, Carly was surprised when Bill threw back his head, laughing heartily.

"I should have figured you'd take the opportunity to pull a few strings while I was gone."

She crossed her arms over her chest. "Marge deserved that promotion, Bill."

"I know," he agreed on a deep sigh. "But it sure was nice while it lasted." He grinned down at her. "If Marge is gone, who tracks down your car keys so you can drive home at night?"

Carly didn't take offense at his teasing tone. "I'm glad you're back, Bill," she said softly. "I've missed you."

Bill put a finger under her chin, lifting her gaze to his. "I've missed you too, Carly. You know you've always been just like a daughter to me. If you ever need anything, I'm right here."

"There is one thing," she offered tentatively.

"Name it," he answered promptly.

Carly's smile wobbled. "I know you're capable of stepping right back into the thick of things, but if you could just give me a bit more time . . ." Her voice drifted off as she realized what she was asking Bill to do.

His laugh was deep and full-bodied. "Don't fret that pretty little head, honeybun. I'll keep your fella in the copilot's seat long enough for him to come to his senses."

Carly knew Bill would do exactly that. While she was admittedly using less than ethical tactics, keeping Patrick in Washington until he realized he loved her, she convinced herself that it was all for the best. After all, when they were celebrating their golden wedding anniversary fifty years from now, this little deception would be long forgotten.

"I love you, Bill McIntyre," she professed, throwing her arms around him.

To her amazement, Bill looked slightly embarrassed at her enthusiastic display. The concern she'd witnessed earlier returned to his eyes.

"Carly, I feel as if I started all this by asking you to convince Ryan to save my spot here at Capitol. If things don't work out . . ."

She pressed her fingers against his lips. "Don't say it," she begged quickly. "If you say a bad thing out loud, it'll come true."

He shook his head. "For an intelligent woman, you sure did absorb some of the funny ideas your grandpappy put into your head. Do you still have that lucky penny?"

Carly pulled it out of her pocket. "Right here."

Bill winked. "Then I guess you've got all the bases covered. That poor fella doesn't stand a chance."

With that he left for his meeting with Patrick. As Carly returned to work, she hoped with all her heart that Bill was right.

That evening, dressed in a pair of red cords and a Seattle Seahawks sweatshirt she had appropriated from Patrick's wardrobe, Carly set the table while Patrick slid two steaks under the broiler.

She had been watching him prepare dinner, finding him every bit as handsome, casually clad in a faded pair of jeans and forest-green wool shirt, as when he was dressed in his expensively tailored business suits. He had rolled the sleeves of the shirt up to the elbows, displaying strong arms that were capable of holding her with heartbreaking tenderness.

How I love him, she thought with a deep, inner sigh. *More than I ever thought it possible to love another human being.*

Unable to resist, she crossed the room and put her arms around his waist. "I envy you."

"I've been hearing that a great deal lately," Patrick responded as he sliced the mushrooms for the salad. "Wherever I go, people are constantly bringing up your name. I'm probably the most envied man in Washington."

Unable to see his face, Carly had trouble reading his casual tone. "I told you people would talk."

Patrick lifted one of her hands to his lips. "If you think I'm concerned about idle gossip, you're wrong, Carly. To tell you the truth, I rather enjoy knowing that men all over the city are eating their hearts out over the fact that I've managed to latch on to the loveliest lady in the land. Not to mention one of the most sought after."

Carly laughed. "You have such a knack for saying exactly the right thing. It must be those well-honed negotiating skills."

"Not at all. It's the truth, and if I've been remiss in telling you how lucky I feel, I promise to begin rectifying that oversight immediately.... But we got off the track," he remembered, lightly leaving her arms to take the olive oil down from a shelf. "Why do you envy me?"

"Because you can cook." She watched as he prepared the salad dressing. "I've tried, you know. I really have." A small, rippling sigh escaped her lips. "But I'm too impatient to follow recipes, and something always goes wrong."

Carly had no proof, but she'd bet her lucky coin that Julia had been a marvelous cook. The kind of woman who could whip up a seven-course meal from a few leftovers and a can of cream of chicken soup.

As he detected the odd little tinge of sadness creeping into Carly's voice, Patrick slowly turned toward her. Putting down the bottle of wine he'd just pulled from the cooler, he covered the slight distance between them and drew her into his arms. Affection was quite evident in his eyes as he looked down at her sober expression.

"Hey, it's not that hard to broil a steak. And since I like to cook, I can't see where we have a problem."

He framed her face in his palms. "Besides, sweetheart, you possess several talents far more appealing. In fact, if you were any more imaginative, I wouldn't be able to crawl out of bed in the morning."

Soft color drifted into her cheeks as Carly thought back to her uninhibited lovemaking after they had returned home that evening. She had practically attacked Patrick, but he hadn't seemed to mind. In fact, he'd seemed quite pleased with her taking the initiative. She was just about to kiss him when a cloud of billowing black smoke caught her attention.

"Your steaks are burning."

"Damn!" Patrick yanked the broiler pan out of the oven and threw it onto the counter. He stared down at the charred fillets. "How do you feel about well-done meat?"

Carly laughed. "It's my favorite kind."

THE SENATOR HAS DECIDED not to retire, after all," Patrick informed her casually during a dinner of scrambled eggs.

"Well, that should certainly take some pressure off you."

"It should. Although for some reason I don't find his tactics to get me to follow in his footsteps nearly as frustrating as I did when I was younger." He gave her a self-deprecating grin. "Perhaps I'm mellowing in my old age."

Carly smiled. Patrick was the most vital, energetic man she'd ever met. He was years away from old age. "I take it he didn't approve of your career goals."

"He hit the roof when I left for Oxford. That was a hard time. I don't know what I would have done without Alex and . . ." His voice drifted off.

Carly reached out, covering his hand with hers on the tabletop. "If you're not saying her name on my account, Patrick, it isn't necessary. Personally, I'm glad you had someone to love you during that time. You and the senator are both incredibly strong-willed men. It must have been difficult."

"It wasn't easy." Patrick fell silent, studying Carly thoughtfully. "You're quite a woman, Carly Ashton," he said finally. "Just when I think you're the world's loveliest scatterbrain, you demonstrate an amazing depth of character."

She rose from the table and settled herself on his lap. "A scatterbrain?"

"Well, you have to admit that your mind tends to skip from thought to thought with blinding speed. The only problem is that you don't always finish one idea before getting carried away with a new one."

Carly slowly unfastened the first button of his shirt. "I'll have you know, Patrick Ryan, that I'm perfectly capable of directing my attention to one thing."

The second button followed. Then the third. "When the subject interests me."

Not taking her eyes from his, she finished the task, pushing the material away. Carly felt him take a breath as she pressed her palms against his naked chest.

"Is that so?" he asked weakly.

"Just watch." She kissed him, tracing a teasing trail from one side of his mouth to the other. When her tongue dampened the skin of his lower lip, Patrick groaned in response.

Encouraged, she bent her head and pressed stinging little kisses down his taut torso.

"Carly," Patrick rasped, "what do you think you're doing?"

She smiled up at him. "I'm seducing you, Patrick." Her hand moved down over his stomach, and her fingers slipped teasingly under his belt. "Is it working?"

Patrick shifted her on his lap, letting her feel the extent of his arousal. "What do you think?" His hand dived under the well-washed sweatshirt to cup her breast.

Her lips trailed up his neck. "I think," she murmured in his ear, before tracing it with the tip of her tongue, "that we're both very talented."

"Talented enough to make love in a flimsy ladder-back chair?"

Carly sighed as his fingers kneaded her flesh. "Though we've been known to be incredibly inventive, perhaps that would be pushing our luck."

His deep chuckle was muffled against her lips. "Who knows—it may be possible. I've been very lucky since arriving in Washington."

Carly's breath mingled with Patrick's as she tasted the wine they'd shared. "It's our lucky coin," she stated absently as her fingers played with the dark hair curling against the back of his neck.

She shared herself so easily, Patrick thought. Alex had warned him from the beginning that Carly merited more than he was capable of giving. She deserved to have the world laid at her feet. He should send her away, back to her own life where she'd meet someone worthy of her. Patrick knew that was the only fair thing to do. And he'd always prided himself on being a fair man.

"Come into the bedroom with me," he urged instead. "I can't wait for you another minute."

She laughed happily. "I thought you'd never ask."

14

WITH BILL BACK at Capitol, Carly found herself with more free time. In addition to the dance class and her frequent benefit performances, she added a Chinese cooking class to her schedule. Since Patrick's expertise in the kitchen didn't extend to Oriental food, Carly was looking forward to surprising him by whipping up a Peking duck.

In reality, Carly knew her skills were a long way from mastering such a complicated recipe. Although her method was enthusiastic, the slices of water chestnuts, scallions and gingerroot never maintained the consistency of size and shape the quick-tempered instructor insisted on. Still, she couldn't help experiencing a sense of pride as she left the class one evening with a foil-wrapped platter of egg rolls. They varied in size and shape, but as she nibbled on one while driving home, Carly decided it was actually quite tasty.

The house was dark as she walked in the door. "Patrick," she called out, putting the platter on the kitchen counter. "Where are you?"

There was no answer. Carly knew Patrick was home; his car was parked out front. Puzzled, she began to search, locating him in the den. A crackling cedar fire provided the only light in the room.

"Patrick?" she asked softly, turning on a desk lamp. The soft glow illuminated his firmly set features. "Is something wrong?"

"Not a thing," he professed. "Why would you think that?"

His cold tone chilled her to the bone. "I don't know. I just thought—"

"I told you," he said firmly. "Nothing's wrong."

"I'm glad." Carly managed a weak smile. "I was afraid you might be ill."

"I'm fine. All right?"

"Sure," Carly agreed without hesitation. "How brave are you feeling tonight?"

"Why?" His tone was not encouraging.

"I brought home some egg rolls."

"I'm not hungry."

They fell silent, the air in the room thick with tension. "Penny for your thoughts," she suggested quietly.

When he didn't answer, Carly sat on the arm of the chair and plucked a coin from behind his ear. "Why, look at this," she stated with mock surprise. "I just happen to have a penny right here."

Patrick jerked away, moving across the room to the window. His hands were jammed into his back pockets as he stared out into the darkness. "I'm not in any mood for your tricks tonight, Carly."

Sighing, she slipped the lucky penny back into her pocket. The silence settled over them once again.

"Alex dropped by to see you tonight," Patrick stated abruptly.

"I wish I'd been here. I like Alex."

"Yeah. He made that perfectly clear."

Carly stared, unable to see his face. "Would you care to explain what you mean by that?"

"Simply that you and he seem to have struck up quite a friendship."

"We were friends long before I met you, Patrick," Carly reminded him quietly but firmly.

"He mentioned a trip you two had planned to Egypt."

So that was it. Carly felt she should be pleased Patrick was jealous, but from his cold, flat tone, she had a feeling that their problem went beyond simple jealousy.

"I've been meaning to talk to him about that," she murmured.

"Oh?"

"It's true I agreed to go, but I've changed my mind. I was hoping he'd understand."

Patrick turned back to her, his eyes mere slits. "What changed your mind? It sounds like a terrific trip. And you could certainly use a vacation."

Carly lifted her chin, refusing to be cowed by his icy behavior. "My work, for one thing."

"The contracts have been ratified, and with Bill back in harness there's no problem with you taking time off," Patrick pointed out all too accurately.

She swallowed. "There's you."

Alex's visit had only served to illustrate to Patrick, once again, how unfair he'd been to her. He had only been thinking of himself from the beginning. Carly was a warm, loving woman. She deserved a man who could give her a home, a family. As much as he wished things were different, he wasn't that man.

"Me?"

Carly stared into the fire as she struggled to keep the tremors from her tone. "Us."

Patrick abruptly dismissed her soft admission. "I told you from the beginning, Carly. There isn't any 'us.' We both knew this was a transitory affair."

Unable to remain still, Carly rose, going over to the fireplace. She poked at the crackling log with the brass poker, watching the scattering of brilliant sparks. Finally, she looked back at him over her shoulder.

"You said you needed me."

Patrick struggled not to give in to the pull of Carly's velvety violet eyes. "I suppose I did. For a time," he agreed, turning away. "I don't anymore." It was the first lie he had ever told her, and Patrick was stunned at how badly it hurt.

Carly's head swam with the realization that Patrick was actually going to let her walk out of his life. "Well, that's certainly laying it on the line," she murmured. "I suppose I should thank you for being so forthright."

When he didn't answer, Carly experienced an urge to fling the poker at his stubborn head. She forced herself to replace it in the rack instead. "Is it standard operating procedure for you to send your women out of the country when you tire of them?"

Even as her sarcasm cut at an exposed nerve, Patrick had to resist the temptation to go to her. "Actually, that's why he dropped by. It seems the Egyptian president is coming to Washington for a state visit, so Alex wanted to let you know that he was going to be forced to postpone the trip indefinitely. He's needed here."

"Oh." Carly decided they were getting nowhere. "That's okay. I didn't really want to go, anyway." She took a deep breath, diving into the murky conversational waters. "And I don't think you really wanted me to leave."

"Carly—"

She shook her head firmly. "We have to get this out in the open, Patrick."

He arched a challenging brow. "Exactly what are you talking about now?"

"The fact that you're so wrapped up in your memories of Julia that you refuse to let anyone else get close to you," she accused daringly.

His eyes smoldered dangerously. "That's ridiculous."

Carly refused to flinch at the banked fury in his eyes. "Is it? She's been standing between us from the beginning. I kept hoping that you'd let her go, that you'd open your eyes and see what we could have together, but that isn't going to happen, is it?"

When Patrick didn't answer, Carly shook her head regretfully. "I never would have taken you for a coward, Patrick."

His glare could have shattered diamonds. She'd hit too close to home with that one. Anger rose quickly, bringing with it pain. A pain he'd think about later, when he was alone. Knowing that he was overreacting, Patrick realized he couldn't remain with Carly another moment without doing something drastic.

"I'm not going to stay here and listen to your ridiculous accusations," he exploded, marching from the room. Moments later Carly heard the front door open and slam behind him, followed by the roar of Patrick's car engine as he drove away.

She waited for him to return late into the night, pacing the floor, her mind going over and over their conversation as she tried to figure out where, exactly, it had taken such a tragic turn. Finally giving up, she went to bed.

Patrick spent the night driving through the darkened streets of the city. He knew he had acted outrageously, just as he knew that he had acted in Carly's own best interests. Although she had been careful not to put demands on him, Patrick was certain that Carly, like all women, desired total intimacy in a relationship.

Whether she would admit it or not, the fact that she had not yet married, despite several attractive opportunities, was proof that she was waiting for one special man: a soul mate to spend the rest of her life with. Patrick had long ago come to the conclusion that such ideas were nothing but romantic illusions. Feeling the way he did, he was definitely not the man for Carly Ashton. She would have discovered that for herself; Alex's visit had only speeded things up a little.

When his friend had first mentioned the Cairo trip, Patrick had tried to think of something, anything, to keep Carly in Washington. By the time Alex had explained that he was forced to postpone the journey, Patrick had realized his motives were entirely selfish. Since he couldn't offer Carly happily ever after, it was only right that she return to her own life. He knew that she was waiting for a declaration of commitment. One that he wasn't able to give. Every day they delayed facing that reality would make it that much more difficult in the end, he told himself firmly.

Patrick returned to the house in the early hours of the morning. As he lay stiffly on his side of the bed, Carly could feel the discomfort still swirling between them. Unwilling to risk another rejection, she feigned sleep.

She was waiting at the kitchen table the next morning, sipping a cup of coffee as Patrick entered the room.

"Good morning," he muttered, going over to the counter to pour his own cup of coffee. Carly, he noticed, hadn't offered.

"Is it? I hadn't noticed."

Instinct told him she was striking back because she was hurting. Who could blame her?

"I've come to a decision," Carly stated suddenly.

Patrick pulled out a chair, straddling it as he fought to keep his expression from revealing his inner turmoil. He wondered when Carly had developed the ability to shield her thoughts so well. Her expression was disconcertingly unreadable.

"About what?"

"You're right. I can't stay here the way things are. So since Egypt is obviously out for the time being, I'm going home."

"To the apartment?"

Carly shook her head. "No. My real home."

Patrick decided that after last night's behavior it would be ridiculous to point out that this was her real home. "I'm having trouble following this."

"It's quite simple, really. I want to get away for a while. I need to lie in the sun and sort things out. Since I still own my grandfather's house in Jacksonville, I decided to go there for a while."

She didn't add that she was hoping that in her absence, Patrick would miss her enough to realize how right they were for each other. How they belonged together.

"What about Capitol?"

He didn't give a damn about the airline at this moment, but he was willing to play on Carly's sense of responsibility to keep her there. As he viewed her lovely face and drank in the sweet scent of white roses, last night's resolve began to slowly crumble.

She shrugged. "I called Bill first thing this morning. He assured me that Capitol can manage without me for a while."

"How long do you expect to be away?"

Carly's dark blue eyes revealed no emotion. No anger, no love, none of the passion she was so capable of feeling. "I don't know."

He took a drink of coffee, trying to corral his whirling thoughts. "I see."

"I thought you would," Carly replied. "You are, after all, an extremely intelligent man." The doorbell chimed and she rose. "That will be my taxi; I have to go."

He stood up as well, putting his cup on the table. "I can drive you to the airport."

She shook her head. "I don't think that would be a very good idea." She brushed a light kiss against his unshaven cheek. "Goodbye, Patrick."

He followed her to the door. Her suitcase was already packed, and he wondered if she'd done it last night or this morning.

"I don't know where you'll be," he objected, wanting to grab hold of her and keep her from leaving. But he knew it was too late. "What if something comes up at the office?"

"I'm certain you and Bill are more than capable of handling things," she responded dryly. She picked up the suitcase and reached for the door handle with her free hand.

Patrick put his hand on her arm. "Carly. . ."

For a fleeting moment, the dark veil over her eyes lifted, and he viewed the blatant hope in there. "Yes, Patrick?" she asked softly.

The doorbell rang again and Patrick dropped his hand. "Enjoy yourself."

Carly didn't answer. Instead she flung open the door, shoved the red suitcase at the taxi driver and ran down the front steps without looking back. She wasn't going to give Patrick the satisfaction of knowing that her heart was shattered.

Patrick stood in the doorway until the taxi turned the corner. *Well, you've done it now,* he told himself harshly. *You've tossed away the only thing in your life that has any meaning.*

THE FIRST THING Carly did when she arrived at her grandfather's house was open all the windows, dispelling the slightly musty odor that indicated all too clearly how long it had been since she'd been home. She roamed the rooms, gaining strength from the memories the small house held for her. It was as if her grandfather's spirit lived on, giving her fortitude when she needed it so desperately. He'd never let her down and as she sat on his bed, eyeing the playbills tacked onto every inch of wall space, she felt the pain that had been gripping at her heart slowly subside.

"It will be all right, won't it, Gramps?" she whispered. "You'll do your magic and make everything all right."

Even as she breathed her heartfelt wish, Carly knew it was going to take more than magic to dispel Julia Ryan's ghost.

Unfortunately, her grandfather had never dabbled in exorcism.

She tried to put Patrick out of her mind as she threw herself into physical activity. She dusted the house from ceiling to floor, waxed every carved swirl on the ancient furniture and polished the stained glass windows until the Florida sunshine created sparkling kaleidoscopes on all the walls. After a week of exhausting labor, the little house was decidedly cheerier. Carly only wished she could say the same thing for herself.

She reached for the telephone several times during those initial days, tempted to call Patrick. But each time she refrained, knowing that she had done all she could. The next move, if there was one, would have to come from Patrick.

PATRICK HAD FOUND Alex waiting for him when he arrived home that first evening. His friend's expression was decidedly formidable.

"What the hell did you do to Carly?" he roared, ignoring the startled gazes of passersby not used to angry scenes in their peaceful Georgetown neighborhood.

Patrick shrugged as he put his key in the lock. "She needed a vacation."

Alex reached out, spinning Patrick back toward him. "Damn you, I warned you not to hurt her!"

Before Patrick could answer that his domestic difficulties were none of Alex's business, his old friend's fist flew out, connecting solidly with his jaw. Stars swam in front of his eyes.

"I should have remembered you were on the boxing team," he muttered, gingerly testing his jaw with his fingers.

"You should have remembered a lot of things," Alex retorted. "The first being that Carly loves you." His black eyes glittered dangerously. "Although why such an intelligent woman should make such a fool of herself over a jerk like you is beyond my comprehension!"

"If that's what you call your friends, I'd love to hear how you talk about your enemies," Patrick muttered, not objecting as Alex followed him into the house.

"She loves you, Patrick."

"I know." He went into the den, where he poured two glasses of Scotch. Tossing back his head, he drained his in a few long, thirsty swallows. "And I love her," he stated, handing one glass to Alex before refilling his own.

"You've got a funny way of showing it, my friend."

Patrick's eyes narrowed. "Then we're still friends?"

Alex sank down onto the sofa. "Of course we are. And that's why I'm not going to sit by and let you screw up the best thing that's ever happened to you." He sipped at the Scotch, eyeing Patrick with ill-concealed frustration. "I thought you had come to your senses when you invited her to move in with you. Obviously, I was wrong."

"That was a mistake."

Electricity practically sparked from Alex as he leaped to his feet and began pacing the room. "You are an idiot."

"On that, we're in agreement."

Alex's dark eyes flashed with irritation. "Do you know what she thinks?"

Patrick shrugged, uncomfortable with this entire conversation. Undeterred by the less than enthusiastic response, Alex continued.

"She thinks that she can't live up to your memory of Julia. She's been browbeating herself because she honestly believes that you're still in love with your first wife."

Patrick groaned, sinking into a chair as he covered his face with his hands. When he finally met Alex's accusing stare, his own eyes were bleak.

"How do you know that?"

"We had lunch together last week. Oh, she tried to pretend everything was perfect, but I finally dragged the truth out of her. I've known Carly long enough to recognize when something's bothering her.... Is she right? Is Julia standing between you?"

Patrick sighed wearily. "In a way. But it's not what she thinks."

Alex put his glass down onto the desk. "You're afraid of losing her. As you did Julia."

Patrick's eyes were bleak. "I couldn't go through that again."

Alex's answer was short and rude. He flung his body into a leather chair, expelling a harsh breath. "Let's attempt to be rational about this. Do you honestly love Carly?"

"Of course. Who wouldn't?"

"Who indeed," Alex murmured. At Patrick's blistering glare, he shook his head. "I don't remember this unfortunate tendency toward jealousy."

"That's because I always knew Julia needed me," Patrick ground out.

"And you think Carly doesn't?" Alex asked incredulously.

"She could get along perfectly well by herself. I've never met such a self-sufficient individual."

"Try looking in the mirror," Alex advised dryly. He leaned forward, his fingers linked between his knees. "Life doesn't offer guarantees, Patrick. Either of you could get run over by a bus tomorrow morning. But there is also an excellent chance that you and Carly could live to a ripe old age. Do you want to spend those years apart because you refused to take a risk?"

When Patrick didn't answer, Alex continued his lobbying effort. "Try picturing how you'd feel if you ran into her at the National Zoo, years from now with a clutch of blond-haired, violet-eyed children in tow. Can you honestly tell me that you wouldn't kick yourself for allowing some other man to win her by default?"

"I don't remember you being so damn logical," Patrick grumbled.

"And I don't recall you ever being a coward," Alex countered.

Patrick dragged his fingers through his hair. "That's what Carly called me."

Black eyes regarded him soberly. "Does it fit?"

"Probably," Patrick admitted gruffly.

"Go to her," Alex advised. He rose, scribbling an address onto the notepad on the desk. He held the piece of paper out to Patrick. "Here's her address in Jacksonville."

"She said she needed time to think," Patrick argued, nevertheless taking the address. "After all, I did rush her into living with me. I owe her some time alone to think things through." He didn't add that he was the one who needed time to sort things out.

"Don't wait too long, my friend."

As Patrick rose to see Alex out, something else occurred to him. "How did you know she'd left town?"

"She called me from the airport and asked me to look after you," Alex answered, increasing Patrick's feelings of guilt even further.

Patrick put his hand on Alex's shoulder as they stood in the open doorway. "Thank you for pointing out what a bastard I've been."

Alex smiled for the first time. "Anytime. After all, what are friends for?"

When Patrick entered the bedroom later that night, something on his pillow caught his attention. Carly's lucky penny. He plucked the tarnished copper coin from the quilted spread, reading its message loud and clear. She still loved him. In stead of feeling buoyed by that idea, Patrick felt even worse.

15

SPRING CAME EARLY to the nation's capital. Patrick's work there was finished. With the airline's financial situation stabilized, there was nothing to hold him in Washington. Still, he found himself unable to return to New York. Instead, he took long, solitary walks, finding that without Carly, her beloved city had lost a great deal of its charm.

The Japanese cherry trees rimming the Tidal Basin were in full bloom, appearing like fluffy pink clouds in the clear blue of the sky. But the sight gave Patrick no pleasure. All he could see was Carly, as he'd viewed her last, her lovely face unnaturally pale, her wide violet eyes dark with pain.

As he passed the days in lonely contemplation, Patrick was stunned by the void Carly had left in his life. With brutal introspection, he forced himself to weigh this empty feeling with the pain he would suffer if he married Carly and something happened to her.

"What difference would it make?" he asked himself as he sat on the steps of the Lincoln Memorial, ten days after Carly's departure from Washington. "Alex is right; she could be run over crossing the street. Would the fact that we weren't together make me hurt any less?"

The answer came to Patrick with the crystal clarity of a mountain stream. Their futures had been unalterably linked since the first time he had seen her; he could no more change that than he could fly to the moon. The simple, overriding fact was that a life without Carly in it, for however long they were allowed, was not a life worth considering.

He rose quickly to his feet, laughing aloud as his decision brought a flood of cooling relief. His obvious good humor brought curious glances from a group of Japanese tourists.

"I'm getting married," he told them happily.

Nodding their approval, the visitors grinned in return. The motor drives of the Nikon cameras around their necks whirred away as they captured the shared moment of enjoyment for posterity.

Early the next morning, as Patrick maneuvered his car through Jacksonville's rush hour traffic, he kept telling himself that he had to have the wrong address. Nothing about the area resembled a residential neighborhood. He continued to check the addresses as he drove past banks, department stores, hotels and office buildings. Just when he was about to give up and call Alex for more specific directions, he found it.

Pulling over to the curb, he stared at the small, turn-of-the-century white stucco house, the sloping roof covered with red Spanish tile. A wide porch flanked the entire front, a throwback to a time when entertainment consisted of watching your neighbors.

Although the tiny house was quaint, it was the surroundings that astonished him. On three sides the small city lot was flanked by miles of asphalt parking lot and a two-story shopping mall. Still disconcerted, he exited the car, made his way up the front steps and knocked.

Carly's heart took a giant leap as she viewed Patrick standing on her front porch. He'd come. Just as she'd wished. There was still magic in this house, after all. Then, warning herself not to expect too much, she attempted a casual tone.

"Hello, Patrick," she stated in a friendly manner, as if it was a common occurrence for him to show up on her doorstep, seven hundred and fifteen miles from Georgetown.

"Hi."

Her gaze swept over him. He looked terrible. There were dark circles under his eyes that were proof of the fact that he'd been driving all night. And his clothes were covered with splotches of dried mud.

"What are you doing here?"

"I came to talk to you."

A car horn sounded loudly just a few feet away. A moment later there was a loud squealing of brakes, then voices raised in argument. The atmosphere was not conducive to conversation. Especially one as important as this.

"May I come in?"

"Of course," she agreed, moving aside to let him enter the front parlor.

The room, like the exterior of the house, was a throwback to another era. A delicately shirred rose satin wallpaper covered the walls, and the furniture was an eclectic collection of what was obviously antiques. Carly sat down on a horsehide sofa, gesturing for him to take a chair across the room.

Patrick hesitated, eyeing the red velvet seat. "I don't know if I should sit down. I'm a little muddy."

A hint of a smile chased across her lips. "So I noticed. What happened?"

"I ran into rain outside Savannah. Then I had the rotten luck to get a flat tire. While I was changing it, some idiot flew by about a hundred miles an hour and I got drenched."

"That was unlucky," she stated, wondering if he had found the penny she'd left for him.

"You're telling me," he agreed. Then he answered her unspoken question. "I guess the penny genie decided that after turning my back on the best thing that's ever happened to me, I didn't deserve any better fortune."

Carly was shaken by the heat gleaming in his eyes. "You'll want to wash up."

"We need to talk."

"We will. But to tell you the truth, Patrick, you look like hell. I think you need a bath, some food and some rest, in that order. Then we'll talk."

"I'd almost forgotten how bossy you can be when you put your mind to it." His slight smile softened his words.

Carly gave him a long, pointed look that didn't give him a great deal of confidence. This could possibly be the toughest negotiating session he had ever encountered.

"It seems you've forgotten a lot of things about me," she countered quietly. Then her tone turned impersonal. "Let me show you the bathroom," she suggested, leading the way to the tiny room at the end of the hall."

"There's no shower."

The complaint was out of his mouth before he could censor his words. Patrick had realized long ago there were two kinds of people in the world. Shower people and bathtub people. While he definitely belonged to the former category, this was no time to argue about something so inconsequential.

"There's a perfectly good bathtub," she pointed out. "However, if you'd prefer, you can stand buck naked out in the backyard and I'll spray you off with the hose."

Patrick was encouraged by her sarcasm. It was a great deal better than the uncaring tone she'd been using since he arrived. He was relieved that Carly was not entirely immune to him.

"In that regard, in case you haven't noticed, your backyard happens to be fifty acres of black asphalt."

"I know that!" Her chin thrust forward, her blue eyes flashing with renewed spirit.

"So what kind of house sits in the middle of a damn shopping mall?"

"The kind that belongs to a woman who refused to sell out to Kingsley Property Management."

Patrick was struck dumb for a long moment, his eyes moving over her face. "Are you serious? You refused to sell and they built the thing around you?"

She folded her arms over her chest. "That's right. Do you have any problems with that?"

Patrick's roar of laughter rang out as the argument dissolved and he pulled her into his arms. "I think it's absolutely perfect. God, how I would've liked to watch you in action."

Carly relented, the stiffness of her body relaxing as she looked up at him, her eyes softening. "I would have liked having you in my corner. I felt a little like David going up against Goliath."

Patrick chose to ignore for the moment that Carly had once accused him of being an advocate for Goliath. "I love you, Carly Ashton," Patrick murmured against her hair.

Her body stiffened instinctively. Carly had never considered herself a timid woman, but she was honestly frightened to death of the upcoming conversation she knew was long overdue.

"Did you bring any clothes?"

Patrick was close to panicking as he heard that impersonal tone return to her voice. "In the car . . . Carly, we have to talk."

She backed away, shaking her head. "Not now. You know I can't think straight until I've had my coffee. And you look exhausted. You need some sleep."

"I'm not going to be able to get any sleep until we get this out in the open," he argued.

Carly held firm. "Take your bath," she advised. "I'll make a pot of coffee and bring you in a change of fresh clothes. Then we'll talk."

He felt like a man who had just gotten a last minute reprieve from the governor. "Thank you, Carly."

It was his formal, heartfelt tone that got to her, disintegrating her defenses. Carly knew it was sheer folly to allow herself to continue to love a man who couldn't stop loving another woman. But she seemed to have no choice. Her heart had dictated her fate, and though Carly still didn't believe in fortune cookies, she had to admit, that one had hit the bull's-eye.

Belatedly discovering that she had run out of coffee, Carly ran down the street to the store, leaving Patrick a note in case he finished with his bath sooner than expected.

The bathtub was deep, the water warm, but Patrick found it impossible to relax. He was facing the most important battle of his life and he still had no idea how to go about it. He had hurt Carly. Hurt her badly. He could only hope that she would give him another chance, even though he had to admit he didn't really deserve one.

He rubbed the washcloth viciously over his body, as if he could scrape away his fears. As he held the cloth over his head, allowing the water to stream over his face, Patrick heard a voice outside the door.

"As you'll see, the bathroom has been restored to its original condition, with the exception of the bathtub. The claw-footed porcelain tub dates to a more modern time, but the architect has located a tin-lined one, which is scheduled to be installed soon."

The door swung opened and Patrick was suddenly confronted by a gaggle of elderly women, all as stunned by his presence as he was by theirs. His hand froze in the air, as his eyes locked with those of the spare, iron-haired leader. Everyone seemed to move at once—the women in front hastily backed out with muffled screams, and at the same time the ones behind pressed forward to see what the commotion was all about. Patrick's hand dropped to cover himself belatedly under the water.

"Carly!"

Carly heard Patrick's roar the moment she entered the house. Throwing the coffee can onto the counter, she raced toward the bathroom, bumping into the cluster of strangers huddled together in the hallway.

"Oh, my God," she cried, "I'd forgotten all about you!" She tried to push her way through the women to the bathroom, already knowing what she'd find.

"Carly!" The yell was repeated with all the ferocity of a wounded lion, and she finally clasped one particularly plump barrier by the shoulders, pulling her out of the way.

"Excuse me," she said breathlessly.

"Hello, Carly." The woman who'd first entered the bathroom greeted her calmly. "It's been quite some time since you were here for our monthly tours.... There's a man in your bathtub, dear."

"Hello, Mrs. Cassidy." Carly nodded. "I know. I heard him roaring."

"He certainly has a strong, deep voice. Is he a professional singer?"

"No."

Mrs. Cassidy was still blocking the doorway as she pursued the subject with all the tenacity of a terrier gnawing on a particularly succulent bone.

"I thought you might have met him somewhere while you were performing," she continued blithely. "If he's not a singer, what does he do for a living?"

While in too much of a hurry to explain Patrick's unique occupation, Carly didn't want to be rude. "He buys and sells companies."

The woman smiled approval. "Oh, isn't that nice! My son has his own company. In Akron."

Carly cast a worried glance at the closed door, but managed a slight smile. "That's nice."

"He makes mudflaps," Mrs. Cassidy revealed proudly. "In fact, most of the trucks you see on the highways use Cassidy mudflaps."

"Goddamn it, Carly, where are you?"

"I'm sorry, Mrs. Cassidy, but . . ." Carly gestured helplessly in the direction of the injured voice.

The elderly woman patted Carly's arm reassuringly. "Of course, dear. Don't worry about us. I'll show the ladies the garden. The azaleas should be in bloom."

She turned, clapping her hands to still the excited murmur of voices. "Ladies, if you'll follow me, we'll explore the grounds."

Carly couldn't resist a fleeting smile at the idea of her tiny backyard, flanked by the asphalt parking lot described as "grounds." Taking a deep breath, she rapped lightly on the door.

"Who is it?" Alarm edged his voice.

"It's me, Patrick. Are you decent?"

"Isn't it a little late to be asking that question?"

She opened the door, allowing herself the unmitigated pleasure of seeing Patrick clad only in a small flowered towel. Even though she had seen him in less, Carly had never before been so aware of what a vibrantly masculine man he was.

His body consisted of perfectly formed muscles that could have been cast in bronze. His legs were long, and when her gaze lingered at the top of them, where he'd covered his body with a garden of blue terry-cloth flowers, she felt a quickening in her own thighs.

"Who the hell was that?" he asked, his irritation causing him to miss the warm desire darkening Carly's eyes.

"The Jacksonville Women's League for Architectural Preservation."

"What the hell was the Jacksonville Women's League for Architectural Preservation doing interrupting my bath?"

Her eyes widened, and try as she might, Carly couldn't hide the dancing lights of amusement. "You were in the tub?"

"I was."

"Stark naked."

"When I'm alone in the bathroom, I'm not expecting to be put on public display."

She leaned against the doorframe, drinking in the sight of his lithe, lean body. "It's not such a bad idea. I've never seen a group of history buffs so excited by the house. We could probably double the price of admission if we made you a featured attraction, Patrick."

As a muscle jerked along his thrusting jawline, Carly realized that thus far Patrick had not found any of this the slightest bit amusing. She reached out, tracing the throbbing line with her fingertips.

"I am sorry. I forgot all about them. I should have let them know I was coming, but it was so sudden."

"What kind of house has old ladies wandering through it?" he asked irritably.

"I'll tell you over breakfast," she coaxed.

"Are *they* going to be hanging around long?"

"They'll be leaving right after they tour the 'grounds,'" she promised.

He lifted a dark brow. "Grounds?"

Carly laughed. "I know. I thought the same thing. But I suppose you've got to do the best with what you've got. And

Mrs. Cassidy's supposed to be showing off the scenic attractions of this place."

Talk about scenic attractions! Her breath caught in her throat as Patrick uncaringly pulled the towel from his lean hips, taking an inordinately long time to fold it neatly over the wooden rack. When he turned back toward her, he cupped his long fingers under her chin, planting a kiss on her lips.

"Just when I think there's nothing you can do to surprise me, you pull another trick out of the hat," he murmured. His knuckles lightly grazed her cheekbone, scattering sparks on her skin. As he pulled her against him, Carly couldn't miss the hard proof of his desire. Needs too long denied welled up inside her.

"You promised we'd talk," she whispered, closing her eyes as his lips trailed a seductive path over her face, first brushing lightly against her chin, her cheeks, finally feathering delicate kisses on her eyelids.

Patrick exhaled a sigh. "I know."

"I do honestly love you, Patrick, but I don't know if there's anything you can say that will convince me this isn't a mistake."

He surprised her by winking, displaying far more self-confidence than he was feeling at the moment. "I've never walked away from the negotiating table a loser, sweetheart, and believe me, I'm not about to begin now."

Carly allowed herself a fleeting glimmer of hope. "I'll get your clothes."

Talking was the last thing he wanted to do with Carly right now. His body had a far more urgent need. "Do you suppose the Jacksonville Women's League for Architectural Preservation has finished touring the grounds?"

Carly couldn't miss the invitation in Patrick's tone or the lambent flame gleaming in his bright blue eyes. "I'm sure they have. As you pointed out, there isn't much to see."

His gaze slowly roamed over her, beginning with the top of her head and moving right down to her pink polished toenails.

"On the contrary," he stated huskily, "the scenery here is unsurpassed."

Carly knew that making love with Patrick would not solve their problem. But she couldn't remember ever wanting anything more than she wanted to be lying in his arms, recapturing the passion they'd shared. Her gleaming eyes took a leisurely tour of his hard body.

"I'd have to agree with you there," she whispered, her gaze returning to his face. "I do so love your body, Patrick."

Unable to resist, she reached out to touch him, placing her hands tentatively on his hips. She watched his expression carefully. Finding no resistance, no withdrawal, she ran her palms slowly up over his stomach, pressing them against his chest where she could feel his heart pounding under her fingertips. When she bent her head to press her lips against his warm skin, Patrick shuddered, revealing that whatever power it was that he held over her, Carly possessed it in equal measure.

"Where's the bedroom?" he asked.

"Across the hall."

Patrick tucked his arm behind her knees, carrying her across the threshold of the bedroom, where he placed her tenderly on the bed. Her eyes were wide and dark, eloquent in their need, and it was all Patrick could do not to take her in one blazing whirlwind of passion. But she deserved more. They both deserved more. He took his time undressing her, using his hands and lips to welcome each bit of newly exposed skin.

Carly closed her eyes, allowing Patrick to lull her into that smoky, half-lit world where reality was suspended and time had no meaning. Where a kiss could last a moment, an hour or an eternity. When her clothes had been leisurely dispensed with, Patrick lay beside her, his elbows on the soft down pillow, his head propped on his hand as his free hand stroked her from her shoulders to her thighs.

"Pansies," he murmured, leaning forward to kiss her, his lips punctuating his words. "Your eyes always remind me of pansies."

Patrick's kisses were restrained, his touch like drifting snowflakes, but Carly could feel the heat building up inside her as if he were setting a torch to her skin. As his fingers trailed up the tender skin of her inner thigh with a liquefying touch, the blood roared in her ears like distant thunder.

Patrick was aware that Carly's unusual pliancy demonstrated her trust in him far more than words could ever proclaim. As much as he wanted her, as desperately as his body ached for release, it was more important that their journey be one of love, not simple sexual hunger.

His hand temporarily abandoned its sensual quest, moving upward to cup her breast, his fingers plucking at its distended tip. A mindless pleasure washed over Carly as she focused solely on the feathery brush of his fingers, the exquisite pleasure of his tongue on her skin. His mouth wandered to her throat as he continued to arouse her slowly, irresistibly.

"I love you," he stated, his words muffled against her skin. "More than life itself."

The roving hand began to move again, across her rib cage, down over her abdomen, feathering its beguiling path down her stomach, then farther still. The distant hum of the traffic faded away to be replaced by the heavy sound of Carly's breathing, her soft, rippling sighs, the low moans that Patrick coaxed forth from her very depths.

He was a wizard, she decided, floating sensuously wherever Patrick chose to take her. He had hypnotized her, cast his spell over her until she could think of nothing but how much she loved him. And how she never wanted to leave his magic realm.

His fingers caressed her intimate flesh, creating a flash-point of need that dispelled her languid mood. Her lassitude shattered like crystal and she cried out, desperately, mindlessly, begging him to take her now.

Her cries melted into Patrick's mouth as he kissed her deeply, his tongue thrusting between her lips in a urgent demand for intimacy. Greedy, she reached to guide him inside her and just as hungrily he obliged, filling her totally, then withdrawing, again and again.

Her nails dug into his shoulders, her hands moved across his back, delighting in the feel of the muscles as they rippled under his moist flesh. They were wild in their need, desperate in their unreasoning passion. Carly captured him in a tangle of arms and legs, matching his fierce rhythm, heatedly, wantonly, as they drove each other headlong into madness.

NOW I BELIEVE IN MAGIC," Patrick murmured much, much later.

Carly gave him a soft smile. "It's about time."

"Marry me," he stated suddenly.

She shook her head slowly, her expression grave. "I love you, Patrick. But I can't change what I am. Not even for you."

"Sweetheart, that's just the point—"

Carly pressed her fingers against his lips. She sat up, pulling the sheets around her. "I've let you set the ground rules for this relationship from the beginning. This time it's my turn to state the terms."

"All right," he agreed, sitting up as well. "Fire away."

She took a deep breath. "I know you loved Julia. And I know how good she was for you. But I can't be the kind of woman she was. I can't promise that I'll ever be anything but a haphazard cook, and you'll probably always have scuffed floors and dust bunnies lurking under the bed."

Patrick arched a dark brow. "Dust bunnies?"

"Dust bunnies." She frowned. "Are you laughing at me?"

He wiped the smile from his face. "Not at all. I've just never heard them called that." He held up his hand in self-defense. "But I promise, I wasn't laughing."

Carly studied him suspiciously. "Good," she stated finally. "To get back to what I was saying, while you might be uncomfortable introducing your eccentric magician wife to all your stuffy New York friends, I promise not to embarrass you by pulling a rabbit out of anyone's pocket or telling my grandfather's vaudeville jokes in public."

"Not that you could ever embarrass me, but that last one is a moot point. I've bought the house in Georgetown," Patrick cut in.

"Don't interrupt me, Patrick," Carly instructed firmly. Her eyes widened as his words sunk in. "You bought the house? Why?"

"I thought you liked it."

"I adore it. But what about your work?"

Unable to keep from touching her any longer, Patrick ran his hand up her arm. "I can set up my office anywhere. I thought you'd want to stay in Washington."

Carly fought the smile threatening to break at any moment. "Aren't you taking a lot for granted?"

Patrick grinned. "You're forgetting, sweetheart, I've got a magic penny. That makes anything possible."

His expression sobered. "I know I acted like a prize jackass. My only excuse was that the more deeply I found myself falling in love, the more I feared losing you."

"And now?" she asked softly.

"Believe me, I've resolved my problems with Julia's death, as well as my feelings about our future. It'll be good, Carly. I promise."

She was so very, very tempted to forego any further discussion. But there were still things she had to say. Points she had to make clear before she could agree to what Patrick was offering. Worried about pushing him into a commitment before he was ready, Carly had been withholding too many of her concerns from Patrick from the beginning. She wasn't about to repeat that mistake.

"You haven't heard all my terms," she insisted sternly, fighting the renewed flare of desire as his fingers trailed across her skin above the sheet. She retrieved the treacherous hand, returning it to the mattress.

Patrick sighed. "Carry on, Carly."

"Life with me won't be as predictable as you might prefer, but neither will it be boring."

"Now that I believe." He couldn't resist leaning over to press a long, lingering kiss against her mouth.

Carly's head spun as she succumbed to the magic of Patrick's kiss, momentarily putting aside her need to get everything out in the open. Finally, before she lost sight of her objective altogether, she forced her mind back to their conversation.

"Now you made me forget," she accused. Her smooth brow furrowed. "There was something else.... Oh, yes. I want to have babies with you, Patrick. Two would be nice, three would be even better."

Carly's trembling hand, as she brushed her bangs out of her eyes, revealed that she was not as much in control as her calm tone might indicate. She took a deep breath before stating her final demand.

"I also insist that you love me. Totally, irrationally, insanely, for the rest of our lives." She linked their fingers together. "As I will you."

Carly met his eyes levelly. "Those are my terms, Patrick And I'm warning you up front, there isn't any room for negotiation. It's a take it or leave it proposition."

Patrick had never loved Carly more than he did at that moment. He breathed a silent prayer of thanksgiving for his lucky stars, Carly's penny or whatever gods had smiled down on him.

"You drive a hard bargain, lady."

She tipped her head in a slight nod. "I had a very good teacher."

Patrick's eyes danced as he grinned down at her. "Next time I think I'll send you up against any obstinate union leaders. You seem to have passed with flying colors."

Carly wasn't about to let Patrick change the subject. Not after it had taken every ounce of nerve she possessed to state her case, knowing it might drive him away, once and for all.

"Well?" she demanded. "I'm still waiting for your answer, Patrick."

Succumbing to the magic Carly was always able to weave around him, Patrick drew her into his arms, unable to remember when he'd ever felt so happy. He pressed his smiling lips against hers.

"Sweetheart, you've just negotiated yourself a lifetime deal."

Harlequin Temptation

COMING NEXT MONTH

#129 FOR THE LOVE OF MIKE
Candace Schuler

Hired to chauffeur sexy Devlin Wingate, Michaelann wasn't about to accept his dinner invitation or get intimately involved. But what could she say when he popped the most important question of all?

#130 THE REAL THING Barbara Delinsky

Within weeks Neil and Deirdre went from being total strangers to volatile roommates. Their love affair, however, had only just begun....

#131 THE PERFECT MIX Cara McLean

Aubrey needed a bodyguard for her purebred cat. Robert came to her rescue. But what he excited in her went far beyond gratitude....

#132 FOR ALL TIME Anne Shorr

Callie was determined to lambaste hotshot developer Michael Brookstone in her newspaper. Until he convinced her they should make love, not war....

ATTRACTIVE, SPACE SAVING BOOK RACK

Display your most prized novels on this handsome and sturdy book rack. The hand-rubbed walnut finish will blend into your library decor with quiet elegance, providing a practical organizer for your favorite hard-or soft-covered books.

Only $9.95

Approximately 16" x 8" when assembled

Assembles in seconds!

To order, rush your name, address and zip code, along with a check or money order for $10.70 ($9.95 plus 75¢ postage and handling) (New York residents add appropriate sales tax), payable to *Harlequin Reader Service* to:

In the U.S.

Harlequin Reader Service
Book Rack Offer
901 Fuhrmann Blvd.
P.O. Box 1325
Buffalo, NY 14269-1325

Offer not available in Canada.

BKR–1

Janet Dailey
Americana

Don't miss a single title from this great collection. The first eight titles have already been published. Complete and mail this coupon today to order books you may have missed.

Harlequin Reader Service

In U.S.A.
901 Fuhrmann Blvd.
P.O. Box 1397
Buffalo, N.Y. 14140

In Canada
P.O. Box 2800
Postal Station A
5170 Yonge Street
Willowdale, Ont. M2N 6J3

Please send me the following titles from the Janet Dailey Americana Collection. I am enclosing a check or money order for $2.75 for each book ordered, plus 75¢ for postage and handling.

_____	ALABAMA	Dangerous Masquerade
_____	ALASKA	Northern Magic
_____	ARIZONA	Sonora Sundown
_____	ARKANSAS	Valley of the Vapours
_____	CALIFORNIA	Fire and Ice
_____	COLORADO	After the Storm
_____	CONNECTICUT	Difficult Decision
_____	DELAWARE	The Matchmakers

Number of titles checked @ $2.75 each = $_____

N.Y. RESIDENTS ADD
    APPROPRIATE SALES TAX $_____

Postage and Handling $___.75____

                            TOTAL $_____

I enclose _____

(Please send check or money order. We cannot be responsible for cash sent through the mail.)

PLEASE PRINT

NAME _____

ADDRESS _____

CITY _____

STATE/PROV. _____

BLJD-A-1

"I also insist that you love me. Totally, irrationally, insanely, for the rest of our lives." She linked their fingers together. "As I will you."

Carly met his eyes levelly. "Those are my terms, Patrick And I'm warning you up front, there isn't any room for negotiation. It's a take it or leave it proposition."

Patrick had never loved Carly more than he did at that moment. He breathed a silent prayer of thanksgiving for his lucky stars, Carly's penny or whatever gods had smiled down on him.

"You drive a hard bargain, lady."

She tipped her head in a slight nod. "I had a very good teacher."

Patrick's eyes danced as he grinned down at her. "Next time I think I'll send you up against any obstinate union leaders. You seem to have passed with flying colors."

Carly wasn't about to let Patrick change the subject. Not after it had taken every ounce of nerve she possessed to state her case, knowing it might drive him away, once and for all.

"Well?" she demanded. "I'm still waiting for your answer, Patrick."

Succumbing to the magic Carly was always able to weave around him, Patrick drew her into his arms, unable to remember when he'd ever felt so happy. He pressed his smiling lips against hers.

"Sweetheart, you've just negotiated yourself a lifetime deal."

Harlequin Temptation

COMING NEXT MONTH

ATTRACTIVE, SPACE SAVING BOOK RACK

Display your most prized novels on this handsome and sturdy book rack. The hand-rubbed walnut finish will blend into your library decor with quiet elegance, providing a practical organizer for your favorite hard-or soft-covered books.

Only $9.95

Approximately 16" x 8" when assembled

Assembles in seconds!

To order, rush your name, address and zip code, along with a check or money order for $10.70 ($9.95 plus 75¢ postage and handling) (New York residents add appropriate sales tax), payable to *Harlequin Reader Service* to:

In the U.S.

Harlequin Reader Service
Book Rack Offer
901 Fuhrmann Blvd.
P.O. Box 1325
Buffalo, NY 14269-1325

Offer not available in Canada.

BKR-1

Janet Dailey
Americana

Don't miss a single title from this great collection. The first eight titles have already been published. Complete and mail this coupon today to order books you may have missed.

Harlequin Reader Service

In U.S.A.
901 Fuhrmann Blvd.
P.O. Box 1397
Buffalo, N.Y. 14140

In Canada
P.O. Box 2800
Postal Station A
5170 Yonge Street
Willowdale, Ont. M2N 6J3

Please send me the following titles from the Janet Dailey Americana Collection. I am enclosing a check or money order for $2.75 for each book ordered, plus 75¢ for postage and handling.

_____	ALABAMA	Dangerous Masquerade
_____	ALASKA	Northern Magic
_____	ARIZONA	Sonora Sundown
_____	ARKANSAS	Valley of the Vapours
_____	CALIFORNIA	Fire and Ice
_____	COLORADO	After the Storm
_____	CONNECTICUT	Difficult Decision
_____	DELAWARE	The Matchmakers

Number of titles checked @ $2.75 each = $_____

N.Y. RESIDENTS ADD
  APPROPRIATE SALES TAX $_____

Postage and Handling $___.75___

                     TOTAL $_____

I enclose _____

(Please send check or money order. We cannot be responsible for cash sent through the mail.)

PLEASE PRINT

NAME _____

ADDRESS _____

CITY _____

STATE/PROV. _____

BLJD-A-1